Sign up to m

when I releas

Join my Patreon (patreon.com/jackbryce) to get early access to my work!

lordjackbryce@gmail.com

Cover design by: Jack Bryce

ISBN-13: 9798300368586

JACK BRYCE

To the Dukes.

Mage of Waycross 2

Chapter 1

I stood on the porch of my property, sipping the last of my coffee and breathing in the crisp morning air. Even after almost a month in Waycross, I still loved every second of it.

Sure, goblins and trolls were skulking in the woods bordering my property, and there was a lot of weird stuff going on, but nothing beats standing on the porch of your own place, free and in control, with nothing but fresh air to breathe and the smell of the trees on the wind.

I loved it.

A sound disturbed my peace. In the distance, I heard the faint rumble of a car engine. I narrowed my eyes and watched the dirt road leading up to my home. Soon enough, Caroline's old sedan came into view, kicking up a small cloud of dust as it pulled into the driveway.

Caroline climbed out, clutching a thick folder of documents to her chest. Even from a distance, I could see her eyes were wide with excitement. She hurried up the path, her red ponytail bouncing with each step.

I waved at her as she hurried my way. "Morning, Caroline," I greeted, smiling at her enthusiasm.

"S-Sean!" she exclaimed, slightly out of breath but grinning. "I, uh, I found something really important. You're not gonna believe this!"

"Good to see you too," I said, chuckling as I gave her a kiss. "Come on in. Let's talk inside where it's cooler."

She flashed me a quick smile, following me into the house. We moved to the living room, and Caroline immediately spread the documents out on the coffee table, her hands moving quickly as she arranged them before she adjusted her glasses. I sat down on the couch, leaning forward to get a better look at what she had brought. Caroline took a seat beside me, her leg brushing against mine in her rush.

"So," I began, glancing at the yellowed papers, "what did you find?"

Caroline took a deep breath, clearly trying to contain her excitement. "I was going through the archives this morning, and I found these old records." She pointed to a particularly worn document. "They mention Jan Vanderlee, one of the town's inhabitants in the late nineteenth century."

I remembered him. He had died as the result of an exorcism after he had been blamed for trying to open a portal to hell. By now, we knew that it likely wasn't hell but rather some other kind of dimension that was home to the goblins. He and representatives of the other major families of Waycross had performed some kind of ritual, trying to open a gate. "Jan Vanderlee?" I echoed. "What's the connection?"

"His remains were buried beneath the ancient oak tree," she said, tapping the paper for emphasis, her eyes locking onto mine. "You know, the one deep in the forest."

I sat back a little, surprised. "Really? Under the oak tree? Why would they bury him there?"

Caroline leaned in closer, her voice lowering slightly. "Apparently, he wanted that, and they somehow saw it fit to fulfill his request, even though the records say the burial was pagan." She paused for a moment, as if making sure I was following.

My curiosity deepened. "Go on," I urged, leaning forward again.

"The documents suggest that the Portal Sigil might be buried with him," she said as she looked at me expectantly.

I sat up straighter, feeling the weight of her

words. "The *Portal Sigil*? Are you sure about this?"

Caroline nodded, her red hair swaying with the movement. "That's what the documents say. He was buried with several belongings, and the records speak of a coin-shaped object of '*grande magicke*' — a talisman of sorts." She let the words sink in for a moment.

I frowned slightly, processing the information. "Do the documents mention anything specific about where exactly under the tree we should look? That's a big area."

Caroline shook her head, her lips pursed in thought. "Not exactly. But they do mention a small stone marker that was placed there. It might help us find the exact spot if it's still there. I figured we could start with that."

I nodded slowly, my mind already turning to the possibilities. "This could be a huge breakthrough, Caroline. If we find the Sigil..." I trailed off, not even needing to finish the thought.

A wide smile spread across Caroline's face, and I noticed a faint blush color her cheeks. "I thought you'd want to know right away, so I just *had* to bring it over. This could be really important."

"Absolutely," I agreed, standing up and running a hand through my hair.

The Portal Sigil… If I could use that, it meant I, too, could open up gateways to other worlds. If anything, Waycross's history had taught me that I would need to be very careful in doing so. After all, that exact thing was what had brought Jan Vanderlee to his end, although I had a suspicion there was something foul about him, and maybe he wasn't altogether undeserving of his fate.

But still, I wasn't eager to follow in his footsteps. But we would need to investigate.

I nodded at Caroline. "Great find! We should check out the area around the oak tree as soon as possible. I think right now, in fact."

I stood up from the couch, my mind racing with the possibilities. The Portal Sigil could change everything if we found it. I looked at Caroline, still seated, her eyes wide with excitement.

"Let's not waste time," I said. "We should head to the oak tree now and start looking."

Caroline nodded, gathering the documents and tucking them back into the folder. "I'm ready when you are," she replied, standing up and smoothing out her skirt.

I paused for a moment. "You know, Daisy might want to join us. She's been really supportive, and I think she'd be interested in this too."

Caroline smiled. "That's a good idea. Let's go ask her."

We headed out of the house and walked to my red Ford pickup truck parked in the driveway. I unlocked it, and we both climbed in. The engine roared to life as I turned the key, and I backed out onto the dirt road that led to Daisy's farm.

The drive was short, and soon we arrived at Daisy's place. Her farmhouse stood surrounded by fields of crops. I parked the truck, and we got out, making our way to the front door.

I knocked, and Daisy answered quickly. She was dressed in jeans and a plaid shirt, her blonde hair pulled back into a loose ponytail.

"Hey, you two!" Daisy said, stepping aside. "What brings you here so early?"

I glanced at Caroline before speaking. "We found something important, Daisy. Caroline discovered old records that suggest the Portal Sigil might be buried under the ancient oak tree, deep in the forest. We're going to investigate and thought you might want to join us."

Daisy's eyes widened. "The Portal Sigil? That sounds incredible! Of course, I'll come with you."

"Great," I said. "We could use your help."

Daisy grabbed a light jacket and followed us back to the truck. Once we were all settled in, I drove the three of us back to my place.

Chapter 2

We returned to my house, and I quickly gathered the tools for our expedition. I grabbed a shovel, my flashlight, my Mossberg 590 shotgun, and my Buck knife. I checked each item carefully, making sure everything was in good condition and that I had plenty of extra slugs in my pockets.

Daisy and Caroline waited in the living room.

When I walked in with the gear, they both looked up eagerly.

"Got everything we need," I said, holding up the equipment.

"I'm ready when y'all are," Daisy added, getting to her feet.

Caroline stood up from the couch. "Perfect. Let's not waste any time."

We headed out to my truck. I secured the tools in the bed while Daisy and Caroline climbed into the cab. Once we were all settled, I started the engine and pulled onto the dirt road leading away from my property.

The drive was quiet, each of us feeling the excitement. I focused on the road ahead, watching the trees thicken as we got closer to our destination. When we couldn't drive any further, I parked at the edge of the forest.

"We'll be walking from here," I said, and the girls nodded their agreement.

We got out and gathered our equipment. The woods were dense here, with barely any sunlight breaking through the leaves overhead. As we walked, twigs and leaves crunched under our feet.

I kept my shotgun at the ready, just in case.

If it wasn't for the excitement I felt racing around in my body, this would have been quite the lovely walk. But as it stood, we were all way too excited for what we might find. Chances were we'd find nothing, but I felt deep down that there was something at that old oak tree — it had always had a certain pull.

After a short hike, we reached the ancient oak tree in its glade. It was massive and gnarly, its trunk wider than I could wrap my arms around. The branches stretched out in all directions, creating a wide circle of shade beneath.

I set down the tools and looked at Daisy and Caroline. "Okay, let's start looking for that stone marker."

We spread out, searching the ground around the tree's base. The roots were thick and twisted, making it hard to spot anything unusual. I used the shovel to clear away some leaves and dirt.

After a few minutes of searching, Daisy called out, "Hey, I think I found somethin'!"

Caroline and I hurried over to where Daisy was crouched near the base of the tree. She pointed to a small stone partially buried in the dirt.

I knelt down to get a closer look. The stone was weathered, but I could make out faint symbols etched into its surface. Somehow, the years had turned its etched side away from the surface. Or maybe all sides had been etched before, and the weather had simply worn down the exposed ones. Either way, I understood now why I had not seen it before.

"This matches the description from those documents," Caroline said, her eyes wide. "We should dig here."

I nodded and picked up the shovel. "Alright, let's get to work."

We took turns digging around the stone marker. The ground was hard, but we made steady progress. After a while, we uncovered a stone lid of sorts. We dug around it for a while until we discovered that it was indeed some kind of lid.

I wiped sweat from my forehead with the back of my hand. "Looks like we found something. Let's check it out."

"There are letters here," Caroline said, pointing out vague markings. "Latin." She focused as if she was reading.

"You know Latin?" Daisy asked.

"I do," she said with a grin before turning back to the stone. "It says, 'Here lies the summoner. Let him rest and never return.'"

"So, it's a doorway," Daisy said.

I nodded. "An entrance to his crypt. But… something feels off. Even more so than normally at this tree. There is some kind of magic at work. It's stronger down there."

"Should we go in?" Caroline asked, and Daisy looked at me too.

For a moment, I hesitated. There were aspects to this that I did not yet understand and could not yet see. And yet, caution wasn't going to solve the problem of goblins and a troll stalking my house. I needed to deal with this.

"I'm going in," I said, "but none of you need to come as well."

"Of course we do," Daisy said without dropping a beat. "At least, I am."

"Me too," Caroline said, her voice resolute.

I grinned at them both, hearing in their voices that there was no room for discussion. They both wanted this, and I felt proud of them for wanting it. "You girls are great," I said. "Come on then."

The lid was heavy, but the three of us managed to lift it together. Underneath was a black opening, a gaping hole of darkness. I turned on my flashlight and shined it into the opening. The beam revealed steps leading to a narrow passageway lined with rough stone walls. Cold air drifted up from below, making me shiver despite the warm morning.

"Stay close," I told Daisy and Caroline. "We don't know what's down there."

With me going first, we carefully made our way down the steps. Our footsteps echoed in the silence. The beam of my flashlight showed the passage stretching on much further than I expected.

Daisy's voice was hushed when she reached the bottom of the steps. "This place is larger than I thought it'd be."

"You're right," Caroline replied. "It's not natural. There must be magic involved."

I nodded, keeping my eyes on the dark path ahead. "Let's keep going."

As we moved further into the crypt, I kept my flashlight steady, illuminating the cold, rough stone walls. The air bit at my skin with an unnatural chill. Eerie sounds echoed from deeper within, making my hair stand on end. The passageway stretched far beyond what I'd expected, with corridors branching off into darkness.

"This place is huge," I said. My breath formed a small cloud in front of me. "It's not like any crypt I've seen before."

Daisy rubbed her arms, her teeth chattering. "It's so cold in here. Something feels off."

Caroline looked around, her eyes wide. "This place has to be magical. There's no way it could *actually* be this big."

I nodded. "You've got that right. This is definitely not normal."

We continued down the passage, our footsteps echoing off the walls. The cold seeped into my bones with each step. Strange noises grew louder — a mix of whispers and distant clatters that set me on edge.

Daisy stopped suddenly. "Look over there. I think I see a bigger room up ahead."

I pointed the flashlight forward. The beam revealed a massive chamber with high ceilings and stone pillars. The air here felt even colder. Eerie creaking sounds seemed to come from every direction at once. Shadows filled the room, obscuring the far walls from view.

Caroline's voice was barely above a whisper. "This is *definitely* not natural."

She was right. No way could there be a chamber this size under the oak tree without magic involved. And even if there could be, a bunch of late nineteenth-century farmers had better things to do than to dig out massive chambers to just bury some guy in. They hardly had time to build a house of stone, let alone a place like this.

I swept the flashlight across the room, noting strange symbols etched into the pillars and walls. "Stay close," I warned. "We don't know what's ahead. If we're dealing with magic, it could be anything."

We stepped into the chamber. The cold air stung my face and hands. I kept the flashlight moving, trying to get a sense of the space. I could not see the far walls; it was that large. The strange symbols glowed faintly, casting an eerie light through the darkness.

Daisy hugged herself tightly. "This place is really creeping me out."

"Yeah, me too," I admitted. "But we need to keep going. The Portal Sigil might be here somewhere."

Caroline nodded. "We should be careful. There could be traps or other dangers."

She was right. This place was big enough even for a few goblins to skulk around in. Reassessing the place in that light, I decided I needed to keep my weapon in a more ready position. I tightened my grip on the shotgun, handing the flashlight to Daisy before raising the shotgun to a low-ready position. "Keep the corridor lit up for me, will you?"

She nodded. "Will do, Sean."

"Okay. Let's stick together and stay alert."

We moved further into the chamber. The flashlight beam revealed more of the strange symbols and markings. With each step, the air grew colder. The eerie sounds intensified. An uneasy feeling settled in my gut, but I pushed it aside. We had to find the Sigil.

As we explored, I couldn't shake the feeling of being watched. The shadows seemed to shift and move on their own. Strange sounds that seemed almost like whispers came from all around us. As we moved, they grew louder, sending a shiver down my spine.

Daisy's voice trembled. "Do you hear that? It sounds like voices."

I nodded. "I hear it. Stay close and keep moving."

Caroline pointed suddenly. "There! I think I see something in that corner."

Daisy swung the flashlight in the direction she indicated. The beam cut through the gloom, revealing three figures stumbling towards us. My breath caught in my throat.

Undead.

Shambling skeletons still wearing the tatters of whatever clothing they had worn in life. They approached with malevolence, bones rattling with each jerky movement. Empty eye sockets stared back at us, filled with an unnatural, faint glow.

"Stay back," I said firmly. "Both of you. Cover your ears."

I heard Daisy and Caroline shuffle backwards, with Daisy providing illumination, craftily putting the flashlight in her mouth as she raised her hands to protect her ears. I raised the Mossberg 590, my palms sweaty against the cool metal. The first skeleton lurched forward, bony fingers outstretched. I took a deep breath, steadying my aim. These things moved slowly, but I shouldn't underestimate them.

I squeezed the trigger. The shotgun's blast echoed through the chamber. The slug tore through the skeleton's ribcage, sending bone shards flying. It crumpled to the ground in a lifeless heap of bones.

But my poor ears… All sound was gone, replaced by a ringing, but I kept focus.

"One down," I muttered, although I did not hear my own voice. I worked the pump, ejecting the casing.

The second skeleton was closing in, its jaw clacking open and shut. I aimed for its skull this time. Another deafening boom, and its head exploded into fragments. The rest of its bones clattered to the floor.

The third skeleton was a few feet away. I took a step back, aiming for the skull. The shotgun roared once more, but the skeleton staggered on — a miss.

"Dammit," I growled. I fired one last shot. The slug shattered the monstrosity's skull, and the skeleton collapsed.

I lowered the shotgun, my breathing heavy. My ears were still ringing, and I took a moment to secure our position, gesturing for Daisy to sweep the place with the flashlight. She did as I asked, and I saw no more immediate threats in this chamber. Still, it was a large chamber, and the creatures could be hidden in the shadows.

But for now, it was clear. As I pushed new rounds into the port — double aught this time, as it would be more effective against these targets — I turned to face Daisy and Caroline as my hearing slowly returned. "Are you two okay?" I asked, my voice a little dull to my own ears.

Daisy nodded vigorously. "That was incredible,

Sean. Where'd you learn to shoot like that?"

"Just practice," I said, shrugging. "And necessity."

Caroline stepped closer, her hand brushing my arm. "Thank you for protecting us."

"Of course," I replied. "But we're not out of the woods yet. Let's keep moving. There might be more of these things around."

We pressed deeper into the crypt. The strange noises continued, seeming to come from all directions at once. We stayed close together, moving cautiously. The chamber stretched on, shadows lurking in every corner. The beam of our flashlight swept back and forth as Daisy remained vigilant.

I kept the shotgun ready, my eyes constantly scanning for any movement. We had to find the Portal Sigil, but staying alive was the priority. This place was full of hidden dangers.

"Sean," Daisy whispered, "do you think there are more skeletons down here?"

"I hope not," I replied. "But we need to be prepared for anything."

As we moved deeper into the crypt, silence surrounded us. My ears still rang from the shotgun blasts, but I kept my focus sharp. The dangers lurking in these shadows were real, and we couldn't let our guard down for a moment.

Daisy held the flashlight steady, its beam sweeping across the cold stone walls and floor. Caroline walked close to me, her eyes darting back and forth, searching for any sign of movement.

"Sean," Daisy said, breaking the silence. "That was amazing. The way you handled them skellies... I don't know what we would've done without you."

I nodded, trying not to let the praise go to my head. "I did what I had to do."

"Still," Caroline added, "your skills are impressive. You've kept us safe so far."

"Thanks," I replied, shooting them both a smile over my shoulder. "But let's keep moving. We'll celebrate later."

As we continued, I noticed the passageway narrowing. The walls seemed to close in on us, and the air grew colder still. My breath formed small clouds in front of me. The strange noises we'd heard earlier persisted, bouncing off the stone walls.

Suddenly, Daisy stopped. Her eyes were fixed on the ground ahead of us.

"Hold up," she said. "Something's not right."

I paused, looking at her. "What do you see?"

She pointed to a flagstone that stood out from the rest. "That tile looks different. It's raised up a bit."

I examined the tile closely. Daisy was right — it was slightly higher than the others. "Good catch, Daisy. That might be a pressure plate. Could trigger a trap."

Caroline's eyes widened. "What should we do?"

I took a step back, considering our options. "We'll need to go around it. Watch your step and follow my lead."

We carefully maneuvered around the suspicious tile. The path was narrow, forcing us to move slowly and deliberately. My heart pounded as we passed the potential trap, but we made it without incident.

Once we were clear, I let out a long breath. "Nice work, everyone. Let's keep going."

The passage opened up into another chamber. I raised my shotgun, ready for any surprises. We stepped inside, and Daisy's flashlight beam revealed more strange symbols covering the walls. The air felt even colder here, and the eerie sounds grew louder.

"Stay close," I said. "We don't know what's waiting for us in here."

Daisy and Caroline nodded. Their faces were tense as we moved forward. The shadows seemed to shift around us, and the glow from the symbols cast weird patterns on the floor.

I kept my shotgun at the ready, my eyes scanning every corner of the room. This crypt was full of surprises, and I wasn't about to let my guard down.

"Sean," Daisy whispered, her voice shaky. "Do you think there are more of them skellies down here?"

"I hope not," I replied, tightening my grip on the shotgun. "But we need to be ready for anything."

"This place is so spooky," Caroline muttered, rubbing her arms. "How much further do you think we need to go?"

I shook my head. "No way to know. It might be much bigger than what we've seen so far if there's magic in place. We just have to keep searching until we find something."

Daisy swung the flashlight around, the beam cutting through the shadows as we proceeded. The light revealed cold, damp stone walls covered in those strange, glowing symbols. Water dripped from the ceiling, creating small puddles on the uneven floor.

"What's that over there?" Daisy asked, pointing to a darker area in the chamber.

I squinted, trying to see what she was pointing at. The light revealed the outlines of five skeletons, each one slowly moving toward us. Their bony hands reached out, and their empty eye sockets glowed faintly. The skeletons' bones clattered against the stone floor as they approached, echoing in the vast chamber.

"More skeletons," I muttered, raising the shotgun. "Same as before. I'll take care of them. Cover your ears!"

Caroline grabbed Daisy's arm, pulling her closer

as Daisy kept her beam on the skeletons, making one swoop for good measure to make sure those five were all that were coming at us. "Be careful, Sean."

I nodded and moved forward, keeping the shotgun aimed at the approaching skeletons. I counted my rounds – seven in the tube, one in the chamber. I had to make 'em count. Having to reload a shotgun with an internal tube magazine under duress was a situation I could cope with but preferred to avoid.

The first skeleton was about ten feet away. I took a deep breath and squeezed the trigger. The shotgun roared, and the skeleton's ribcage exploded into shards of bone. It crumpled to the ground, lifeless. Once again, the bang reverberated through the chamber, removing my hearing, but I expected it and knew how it would be, so it didn't faze me.

I worked the pump, ejecting the spent shell. The next skeleton was closing in. I aimed for its skull and fired. The blast shattered its head, and it collapsed in a heap.

Two down.

I pumped the shotgun again, turning to the third skeleton. I aimed for its chest and pulled the trigger. But this one staggered on, and I quickly realized I had missed my shot. "Shit," I hissed, working the pump again.

The skeleton was almost on me. I aimed and pulled the trigger. Another miss. I could have sworn it was a hit, but then again, a skeleton is more difficult to hit than a man. There's a lot of space between those bones…

"Sean!" Daisy shouted, but it sounded like a dull whisper. "Look out!"

Panic surged through me as I pumped the shotgun again. I fired at the skeleton, and the buck tore through its collarbone. It fell to the ground in pieces. Three down.

The fourth skeleton was right behind it. In a quick action, I aimed for its hips, hoping to slow it down. The shotgun roared again, and the skeleton's hip shattered. It toppled forward, dragging itself toward me. I aimed at its head and fired. The blast obliterated its skull, and it went still. Four down.

I turned to the fifth skeleton. It was only a few

feet away. I aimed for its chest and fired the last round. I hit the thing in the skull, and the skeleton crumpled to the ground.

I lowered the shotgun, breathing heavily. My ears were ringing, and my hands shook from the adrenaline. I had emptied the shotgun, and I quickly fished some rounds from my pocket and pushed them into the loading port one by one. Luckily, the movements were all muscle memory, so I could keep my eyes on the chamber, making sure no new threat shambled our way.

"Daisy, Caroline," I called out over my shoulder, my voice barely audible to myself. "It's clear. You can come forward."

They hurried over, their faces pale in the dim light.

"Sean, are you alright?" Caroline asked, her hand on my arm.

"I'm fine," I replied. "But I need to reload."

I quickly finished reloading the shotgun, my hands moving with practiced efficiency. I was grateful for all the time I spent at the range and practicing with all kinds of firearms. I hadn't really expected I would need those skills like this, but it certainly paid off.

Once I was ready, I turned back to the girls. "Let's hope this was the last of them," I said. "I don't have infinite ammunition to deal with these nasties."

The girls nodded, and we continued through the corridor, the air still cold and filled with strange sounds. The walls seemed to close in around us as we moved deeper into the crypt. The magic in the air seemed to be growing thicker, and I was hoping we would reach our destination soon.

As we moved, I spotted another chamber ahead. "Let's check it out," I said, motioning to Daisy and Caroline.

We entered cautiously. The room was larger than the others we'd seen. In the center stood a massive stone sarcophagus. Its lid was carved with the image of a man in a cloak, lying still.

Caroline stepped closer to the sarcophagus. Her eyes widened. "This has to be it," she said. "Jan Vanderlee's final resting place."

"How can you tell?" I asked.

She ran her hand over the carvings. "These match the descriptions from the old documents –

the reports from the sheriff. The clothing, the pose – it's all as they described. But... I didn't think they would have made such an elaborate resting place for him."

"I don't think they did," I said, studying the sarcophagus. "This was magic."

Daisy shone the flashlight over the stone coffin. "What do you think, Sean? Should we open it?"

I examined the sarcophagus closely. Four metal clasps held the lid firmly in place. "We'll need to break these first," I said, pointing to the clasps.

Caroline turned to me. "Can you use the Metal Sigil?"

I nodded, summoning forth the Sigil book after handing Daisy the loaded Mossberg. "I'll give it a try. Keep watch while I work on this."

Daisy and Caroline stepped back, their eyes darting around the chamber. Daisy kept the shotgun in a good ready position, showing me she was comfortable with firearms as well. Perhaps her father or one of her mothers had taught her. Once I held the book, I felt the familiar rush of mana in my channels. Focusing on the clasps, I willed them to break.

At first, nothing happened. Then, with a groan, the first clasp snapped open. One by one, the others followed suit.

"It worked," I said, stepping back from the sarcophagus. "Help me push the lid off."

The three of us positioned ourselves around the stone coffin. "On three," I said. "One, two, three!"

We pushed with all our might. Slowly, the heavy lid slid to the side, revealing the contents within. The smell of musty air and decay wafted up, making me wrinkle my nose.

Inside lay a skeleton, its bones yellow with age. In its bony hands, it clutched a purple, coin-shaped object. As with the other Sigils, markings were etched into it, and I felt a magical pull from its energy. It resonated with me. Jan Vanderlee's downfall — his secret magical object.

My heart was racing. What magical world would open to me if I learned to use this?

Caroline leaned in for a closer look. "That's it," she whispered. "The Portal Sigil."

Daisy's flashlight beam illuminated the skeletal remains and the Sigil. "Amazing," she muttered before glancing at me. "Won't you claim it?"

"Yes," Caroline agreed. "Take it, Sean."

I nodded and reached out. As soon as my fingers touched the Portal Sigil, a surge of energy shot through me. It felt like being struck by lightning, but instead of pain, there was only raw power. My whole body tingled, and for a moment, I thought I could sense every particle in the air around me.

"Whoa," I gasped, quickly shoving the Sigil into the third and final slot of my book and snapping it shut. The sensation dampened, but I could still feel its presence, like a low hum in the back of my mind.

"What happened?" Daisy asked, her eyes wide with concern.

I shook my head, trying to clear it. "Nothing bad. Just... intense. We need to get out of here."

Caroline nodded, her face pale in the dim light. "Agreed. Let's go."

We gathered our tools and began retracing our steps through the crypt. The air felt colder now, and the shadows seemed to move at the edge of my vision. I gripped my shotgun tightly, keeping it ready.

"Watch your step," I warned as we navigated the narrow passageways. "And keep an eye out for any more of those skeletons."

Daisy swept the flashlight beam back and forth, illuminating the rough stone walls. "Do you think there are more?" she asked, her voice barely above a whisper.

"I hope not," I replied. "But let's not take any chances."

We passed the chamber where we'd fought the skeletons earlier. Their bones lay scattered across the floor, a reminder of our earlier battle. Caroline shuddered as we walked by.

"I can't believe we made it through that," she said.

"We're not out yet," I reminded her. "Stay focused."

As we approached the narrow passageway with the raised tile, I held up a hand to stop the others. "Remember the trap? We need to go around it carefully."

One by one, we edged past the suspicious tile, pressing our backs against the cold stone wall. I held my breath, half-expecting something to spring out at us, but nothing happened.

Finally, we reached the steps leading up to the entrance. I climbed first, shotgun at the ready, and pushed open the heavy stone lid. Sunlight streamed in, momentarily blinding me after the darkness of the crypt. It felt like emerging from some strange kind of dream and back into reality.

I blinked rapidly, scanning the area around the ancient oak tree. "It's clear," I called down to the others. "Come on up."

Daisy and Caroline emerged, squinting in the bright light. We all took deep breaths of the fresh air, the musty smell of the crypt still clinging to our clothes.

Eager to leave, we hurried to my truck, tossing the tools in the bed before climbing into the cab. The familiar rumble of the engine was comforting after the eerie silence of the crypt.

As we drove back to my place, Caroline turned to me. "Sean, what did it feel like when you touched the Sigil?"

I thought for a moment, trying to find the right words. "It was like... being connected to something supernatural. Powerful, but overwhelming."

"Do you think it's dangerous?" Daisy asked from the backseat.

"Could be," I admitted. "That's why we need to be careful with it."

The girls both nodded in agreement. Still, they grinned broadly, and I noticed that I had been doing the same. My hands were shaking a little as I gripped the steering wheel. This had been a *real* adventure – something above and beyond the things any of us had ever experienced. I felt that it strengthened our bonds, made us stronger, and that it was the beginning of something new.

A moment later, we began talking – full of excitement – about what we had just done, what we had seen, and about the new world that was opening up to us.

Chapter 3

We returned to my house as the sun was setting. My home stood silent against the darkening sky. Inside, the familiar smell of aged timber greeted us. Excited, we gathered in the living room, where I placed the Sigil book on the coffee table, while Daisy went into the kitchen to get us drinks.

I sat down on the couch and opened the book to

the page that contained the Portal Sigil. Its purple surface caught the last rays of sunlight slanting in through the windows. It shimmered faintly, almost alive. As Daisy placed a glass of sweet lemonade on the table for each of us, she and Caroline sat on the couch beside me, their eyes fixed on the book.

"So," I said, looking at the Sigil, "we've got it. But we need to figure out what it does."

Caroline nodded. "You're right. We can't risk activating it without understanding its potential. It could be dangerous."

I nodded slowly. I understood her caution, but there was curiosity burning deep within me. I really wanted to see what I could do with it.

"What do you think it might do?" Daisy asked. She leaned forward, her gaze never leaving the Sigil. "Open portals to other worlds?"

I scratched my head. "Maybe. And it closes them, if the history of Waycross is to be believed. After all, the first settlers — George Blake among them — used it to *close* a gateway, while Jan Vanderlee was accused of using it to *open* one."

"Well, we would need to be sure," Caroline

said. "We can't afford mistakes with something this powerful."

"There isn't much to research, though," I said. "All sources we have do not cover the magic itself or how it works."

"Could we experiment with it?" Daisy suggested. "We could try a small activation. Just to see what happens. But we should be ready for anything."

I smiled and nodded. Daisy was like me in that way — a little more rash than Caroline was. I could imagine a country upbringing would do that to a girl — less bookish and more adventurous. I loved them both in their own way, but I was on Daisy's side with this.

"I'm not sure," Caroline hummed. "It might be dangerous."

I nodded slowly, and Daisy turned to me. "What do you think, Sean? Should we try it?"

The truth was, I wanted to try like she did, but I was not going to do so with both of them in my immediate presence. If there was a risk to it, then I — as the burgeoning mage eager to learn all of this — would bear that risk on my own. They had already done a lot by coming into Jan Vanderlee's crypt with me, and I was not going to expose them to magical experimentation.

I took a deep breath. "Let's not rush. We need to be absolutely sure we're ready."

Caroline nodded. "I can keep looking in the library. There just might be more information on the Sigils, even if it's cursory."

"Good idea," Daisy said. "So long as we don't see any more of them skellies, I'll be fine!"

I chuckled at that, and so did Caroline. After that, we kept talking about our plans and about the potential of this new magical Sigil. I felt glad to have Daisy and Caroline with me. We were facing unknown dangers together, but we were determined to find answers. I had a feeling that they would not lightly step back from this adventure but were in it for the long haul with me, and that pleased me greatly.

We ate a late dinner, prepared over the restored stove in my kitchen, but the conversation continued unabated. We were all swept up by this fantastic idea that there were magical worlds beyond our own — worlds we might get to see. I hadn't felt this kind of excitement since I'd been a kid, fantasizing about magical realms or being a space explorer and getting to see many different places.

After the meal, as night fell, the excitement waned a little, and we all started to feel tired. Caroline yawned. "Maybe we should stop for tonight," she said. "We've made great progress, but we need rest."

"Yeah, I'm exhausted," Daisy agreed. "Let's continue tomorrow."

I stood up and stretched. "Alright. We'll pick this up in the morning. Time for sleep."

We cleaned up the living room, putting away all the books and papers. I carefully placed the Sigil book on a high shelf. I could still see it, but it was out of easy reach. Caroline and Daisy went upstairs to get ready for bed, having decided they would both spend the night — to my great pleasure. I heard the old wooden stairs creak as they climbed, and it felt great to share my house with women I loved. I locked the front door, set the alarm, and checked all the windows to make sure everything was secure.

Once the house was quiet, I sat back down in the living room. The day's events weighed heavily on my mind. The lamp's light cast long shadows across the room, playing over the old wooden walls. I wanted to join my girls, have a little fun with them, but the Sigil seemed to beckon me — to call me. I didn't want to wait too long with experimenting with it — I was just too curious.

I knew I had to try it out. Waiting until morning felt impossible.

I stood up and walked over to the shelf, taking down the Sigil book. The dull surface of the book reflected the lamp's light, and I felt a surge of energy just looking at it. I took a deep breath and opened the book, placing the Portal Sigil alongside the Wood and Metal Sigils. As soon as it was in place, I felt a hum of power flow through me.

Feeling the raw might, I took the book and sat down at the kitchen table, the wood cool beneath my arms. The house was quiet, and the whole world seemed to hold its breath as I prepared to once again use this item that had lain underground for more than a century. I closed my eyes and focused on the Sigil. I imagined a portal opening before me, picturing it in my mind. The air around me grew colder, and a strange tingling sensation spread through my fingers.

When I opened my eyes, a faint, shimmering light had appeared in front of me. It grew brighter and more defined. Slowly, a small portal began to form. Through the opening, I could see glimpses of another world. Dense forests stretched out as far as the eye could see, and patches of shining rock glinted in the sunlight. The colors were vibrant, almost unreal, and it took me a moment to realize that those rocks were almost pure metals.

A fantasy world…

I leaned closer, my nose nearly touching the edge of the portal. The other world looked inviting and mysterious at the same time. The trees swayed gently, and I could almost hear the rustling of leaves. Those strange deposits of metals sparkled as the moonlight hit them, hinting at untapped resources.

"I can't believe it," I whispered to myself. "It actually worked."

My heart raced as I considered the possibilities. But I knew I had to be careful. I had no idea what dangers might be lurking beyond the portal.

"Okay, let's close this up," I muttered, focusing on shutting the portal. "See if this works too…"

As I focused my mind on sealing the portal again, the shimmering light began to fade, and the portal slowly shrank until it disappeared completely. I sat back in my chair, feeling a mix of excitement and nervousness. Both closing and opening the portal had taken a significant amount of mana, and I felt that I had no control over where the portal actually went. The power of the Portal Sigil was incredible, but I needed to be cautious — there was a lot unpredictable about it.

I stood up, my legs a bit shaky, and walked back to the shelf. I closed the Sigil book and placed it back, making sure it was secure. My mind was buzzing with thoughts of the other world I had seen.

"I can't keep this to myself," I said quietly. "I'll have to tell the girls in the morning."

I turned off the lamp, plunging the room into darkness. As I headed upstairs, my mind was still racing. The wooden steps creaked under my feet as I climbed. I paused at the top, looking back down at the darkened living room.

"Tomorrow's going to be interesting," I muttered to myself before heading to join the girls in bed.

Chapter 4

The next morning, I woke up early. My mind was racing with thoughts of the portal I'd opened the night before. The image of that other world was clear in my memory. I needed to tell Caroline and Daisy about it.

I looked over at them, still asleep in bed. Their faces were peaceful. I decided to let them rest a bit longer and headed downstairs to make coffee.

The kitchen was quiet as I brewed a pot. The smell of coffee filled the air, and the familiar scent of this morning ritual grounded me a little and helped me temper my curiosity — at least, until the girls would be down. I poured myself a cup and sat at the table. I sipped my coffee and thought about what I'd seen through the portal.

A few minutes later, I heard footsteps on the stairs. Daisy and Caroline walked into the kitchen, rubbing their eyes.

"Morning, Sean," Daisy said. She yawned. "You're up early."

"Yeah," I said. I couldn't hide my excitement and hopped to my feet, pouring them both a mug of coffee. "And I've got something to tell you both. Sit down, please."

They joined me at the table. I poured them each a cup of coffee. Caroline took a sip and looked at me.

"What's going on, Sean?" she asked. She set her cup down.

I leaned forward. "Last night, after you two went to bed, I tried out the Portal Sigil. I wanted to see what it could do."

Caroline's eyes widened. "You did? Wasn't that… Wasn't that dangerous?"

"Maybe," I conceded. "But I need to experiment with these powers, Caroline, and I wanted to do it alone to make sure that I wouldn't jeopardize you two."

"Aww," Daisy hummed, placing her hand on my forearm while giving me those big, blue lookers. "That's sweet of you, Sean."

"Y-yeah," Caroline agreed. "But dangerous."

"Magic *is* dangerous, Caroline," I said. "We have no access to written records or other information to help us along with this thing. It is what it is, and there will be risks involved in experimentation. I think it's very sweet that you're concerned for me, but I take calculated risks, and it's necessary to do so, so I can make sure we're all as safe as we can be."

Caroline nodded slowly, seeing my point but not necessarily liking it. Daisy was already there, shooting me a broad smile. "Well?" she asked, almost hopping in her chair with excitement. "What happened? Tell us everything." She leaned in closer.

I took a deep breath. "I focused on the Sigil, and a portal started to form. It was small at first, but then it got bigger. Through it, I could see another world."

"What did you see?" Caroline asked.

"There was a dense forest," I said. "And patches of iron ore in the ground. The colors were so bright. It looked real, but different from our world."

Carline smiled broadly. "Sean, that sounds amazing. Iron and wood. Could it be because it is near or somehow associated with the Wood Sigil and the Metal Sigil?"

That was very astute of her. I nodded enthusiastically. "Yeah, could be they're working together in some way. We can't ignore this. We have to explore it. I want to go in there — see what that world is all about."

Daisy put her hand on mine. "Sean, we understand. But you're not going alone. We're coming with you."

"She's right," Caroline said. "We need to stick together. We can help each other stay safe."

I looked at them both. At first, I hadn't wanted to risk them, but I realized now that keeping them out of it all was just as unfair. After all, they had greatly enjoyed yesterday's expedition to the crypt. They wanted more, and I would love to have them with me. Sure, there were risks, but if I kept a cool and level head, I would be able to protect them. Besides, they had some skills themselves. I was pretty sure Daisy was a mean shot, and Caroline was perceptive and intelligent.

With a smile, I grabbed their hands. "You girls are the best," I said. "I'm very glad you want to come. But we need to be prepared. We can't just jump into this without the right supplies."

Daisy smiled. "You're right. We'll need food, ammo, and extra gear. I think I should get a weapon too. I know how to use one, and it'll make me feel safer."

"I was thinking the same thing," I said. "We'll go into Waycross, pay a visit to Earl's, and get everything we need. We'll make sure we're ready for whatever we might find."

We finished our coffee and got ready to go into town. I grabbed my keys, and we headed out to my red Ford truck. We climbed in, and I started the engine.

As we pulled up in front of Earl's store, excitement buzzed through my body. The old building stood before us, chairs arranged on the porch, and the sign dangling above the steps leading up. This familiar spot was about to become the starting point for something extraordinary. I parked the truck, and we got out, ready to gather our supplies.

We were all buzzing with excitement, looking forward to undertaking this expedition to a brand-new world, and there was a bounce to my step as I pushed open the door, triggering the bell above. "Morning, Earl," I called out.

Earl looked up from behind the counter, his face brightening. "Well, if it ain't Sean. And Miss Daisy and Miss Caroline too! What brings y'all in today?"

I walked up to the counter. "Morning, Earl. We need to stock up on a few things."

"Sure thing," he said, stepping out from behind the counter. His boots thudded on the wooden floor. "What can I get for ya?"

"First off, we need some ammunition. For the Mossberg mainly," I said. I gestured toward Daisy. "And Daisy here wants to get herself a shotgun."

Earl's eyebrows shot up. "Daisy, you lookin' to get armed, huh? What's the occasion?"

Daisy stepped forward. "Just wanna be prepared, Earl. You know, after what happened to Timothy Harton's cattle, we figured it's best to be on the safe side."

Earl's face grew serious. "Yeah, that was somethin'. Nasty business." He paused, then nodded. "Alright, y'all follow me."

He led us to the back of the store. A modest collection of rifles and shotguns lined the walls. Boxes of ammunition filled the shelves below. Earl reached up and pulled down a shotgun from the rack. He handed it to Daisy.

"This here's a Remington 870," he said. "Good all-purpose shotgun. Reliable and sturdy."

Daisy took the shotgun. She checked its weight, then brought it up to her shoulder. She nodded. "Takes 12-gauge like Sean's?"

"That it does," Earl said with a grin, shooting me a wink that conveyed 'gotta love a woman who knows her firearms.'

I grinned, sharing the sentiment.

She inspected the weapon a moment longer, working the slide and inspecting for damage until she gave a satisfied nod. "This'll do nicely. Thanks, Earl."

"No problem," Earl said. He turned to me. "How much ammo you lookin' to get, Sean?"

I thought for a moment. "Let's start with a couple of boxes of slugs. And maybe some more double-aught buckshot too." I reckoned that the buckshot might be more effective against the skellies, as I was pretty sure that some of those slugs had just gone between ribs or bones. A nice spread would prevent that, and we were engaging them at close range anyway.

Earl grabbed the ammunition and handed it to me. The boxes were heavy in my hands. "Anything else y'all need?"

Caroline spoke up. "Yeah, we, uh, we need some provisions. Canned goods, water, and maybe a first aid kit."

Earl nodded. "Alright, let's head back to the front. Got all that stuff up there."

We followed him back to the front of the store. Shelves lined the walls, packed with various goods. Earl began gathering the items we needed. He piled them on the counter.

"So, you three goin' on some kinda adventure?" Earl asked as he worked. His eyes sparkled with curiosity.

I hesitated. I couldn't tell him the whole truth. There was a lot of risk involved, and I didn't want the word getting out that I was a practitioner of magical arts. People wouldn't understand, and I was certain some kind of authority would become involved.

Not what I wanted.

"Just want to be prepared, Earl," I said. "You know how it is."

Earl chuckled. "Sure do. Better safe than sorry." He paused, his expression growing serious. "That business with old Tim's cattle... well, can't blame ya for wantin' to be ready. Looks like there's some mighty mean critters out there. More than just your regular mean critters." He thought for a moment, reaching some kind of conclusion in his own way.

I had by now come to understand that Earl was the type of man who wasn't a fast thinker, but a thorough thinker. He came to his conclusions, and they were often right. But he took his time to get there, and that was a good thing.

"Waycross has always had its share of weirdness," he said pensively, looking me over. "But I won't stick my nose where it don't belong."

I smiled and nodded. "It's a unique place, alright," I agreed. "Thanks."

He grinned. "Think nothin' of it."

As Earl rang up our purchases, Daisy and Caroline whispered to each other. They checked over our supplies, making sure we hadn't forgotten anything. I pulled out my wallet and paid for everything. I still had plenty of money in the bank, and I was grateful for that. The early retirement I had invested in and saved for was turning out to be a lot more exciting than I had thought, though.

We carried our supplies out to the truck. The sun beat down on us as we loaded everything into the bed. Earl stepped out onto the porch. He watched us, his brow furrowed.

"Y'all take care out there, alright?" Earl called out.

I looked up at him. "We will, Earl. Thanks for your help."

"Anytime, Sean. Y'all come back if you need anything else."

We climbed into the truck. Our supplies sat securely in the bed. I started the engine and looked at Daisy and Caroline. Daisy held her new shotgun close. Caroline's eyes were fixed on the road ahead.

"Ready to head back?" I asked.

Daisy nodded. "Ready."

"Let's do this," Caroline said.

I pulled out onto the road. As we drove back to my house, my mind raced. The portal awaited us.

Chapter 5

As the truck bounced along the dirt road, Daisy held her new shotgun close. Caroline stared ahead, her eyes fixed on the road. In the back, our supplies rattled with each bump.

"When we go in there," I began, wanting to review tactics with my women, "I will take point, and I want Caroline in the middle and Daisy closing our formation. If we're in a cramped space or entering a chamber, then Daisy should be right behind me with her Remington instead, and Caroline should stay back until the room is cleared. When we clear a room, I will buttonhook to the right, and Daisy to the left. Think we can manage that?"

Both girls gave confident nods, and Daisy seemed to be looking forward to the action. I smiled and nodded. "Excellent," I said. "We'll be veteran adventurers in no time!"

A moment later, my house came into view, standing out against the dense woods. I pulled into the driveway and turned off the engine.

"Let's get everything inside," I said. I opened my door and hopped out.

Daisy and Caroline followed. We unloaded the supplies from the truck bed. The air was crisp and cool against my skin as we worked. The idea that we were about to head into some kind of magical portal felt almost overwhelmingly unreal. But I knew the truth of the Sigils, and I expected that this would be the start of an adventure that would challenge my perception of reality.

The girls seemed to be occupied with similar thoughts, and we shared excited and wide-eyed glances as we carried the supplies into the house, setting them down on the kitchen table. The old wooden floors groaned under our feet as we worked, and the familiar smell of aged timber – now the smell of home – filled my nostrils.

"We need to pack efficiently," I said. "We don't know how long we'll be gone. Each of us will take a ruck and fill it with ammunition and supplies. We're not going to pack a tent, as I'm counting on being able to either find shelter or teleport us back when we get too tired."

Daisy nodded. "I'll handle the food and water." She opened a box and started organizing canned goods and water bottles into backpacks.

Caroline sat at the table. "I've got the medical supplies," she said. She unpacked the first aid kit.

I grabbed the ammunition. I loaded extra shell holders for both shotguns. "Once we're packed, we'll go over the plan again," I said.

We worked as the sun rose higher. All three of us had plenty of experience hiking, so it didn't take us too long to pack our stuff the right way.

Daisy finished with the food and water. Caroline organized the first aid kit. I had finished my own pack and checked our ammo supply.

"Alright," I said. I stood up straight and stretched. "Let's review. Daisy, food and water?"

"All set," she replied. She patted her backpack.

"Caroline, medical supplies?"

"Ready," she said. She zipped up the kit and secured it in her pack.

I checked the ammunition one last time. "Okay, we're ready. Let's have a quick lunch and then get ready for this adventure!"

Caroline and Daisy exchanged excited glances, and we quickly prepared a simple but sustaining lunch of meat, sandwiches, and fruit — something to keep us moving for a couple of hours. As we ate, we speculated about the magical realm we were about to explore, wondering about the types of creatures we would run into.

"Will it be just like here?" Caroline asked. "Or will we see really strange things?"

"I'm not sure," I said, "but the forest seemed familiar enough, much like the forests we have here, so I'm not sure if it's going to be *that* different."

"Maybe I can bring back some real power crops," Daisy joked. "I wouldn't mind better cereal crops."

As we chatted and finished up lunch, we moved to the living room where our packs and weapons were waiting on us. I retrieved the Sigil book from the high shelf, and the potency of the magical Sigils within set the hairs on my arms on end. I opened it to the Portal Sigil page. Power hummed through me.

I took a deep breath and looked at each of the girls in turn. "So," I said, "are you ready?"

Daisy clapped her hands and gave an excited little hop. "More than ready!" she said, and I could see the radiance in her expression; she meant every word of it.

Caroline was a little more careful, but she still looked ready and firm, giving me a solid nod. "Ready," she said.

I took a deep breath. "Alright, then this is it." Shotgun in one hand, book in the other, I turned to the center of the living room. "Stay close," I said. I looked at Daisy and Caroline. "I'm opening the portal now."

They nodded, faces serious. Daisy had her Remington at the ready, and Caroline stood a step or two behind her. I focused on the Sigil and pictured the portal in my mind. Within a moment, the mana was thrumming in my channels, spreading its potent power, and my fingers tingled. A faint light appeared. It grew brighter, more defined.

Then, a small portal formed.

Through it, I once again saw dense forest and patches of iron ore. The colors were bright and inviting, as if this world was somehow a more vibrant version of our own. The need to explore it surged within me as Daisy and Caroline muttered their wonder behind me.

"It's… wow…" Daisy hummed.

"Amazing," Caroline whispered. "I can't believe it."

"Believe it," I said, smiling at them over my shoulder. "Let's go." I stepped forward, eager to be the first through the gate. Daisy and Caroline followed close behind. Their backpacks were secure, and Daisy held her shotgun ready.

We stepped through. The world shifted, and my living room faded away, making room for someplace else entirely. A second later, we stood in a new world. Thick forests surrounded us. The ground sparkled with surface iron ore. There seemed to be more iron ore here than regular stone.

But like in our own world, there was a yellow sun overhead. It was cool under the trees, but a summery scent and warmth lingered in the air. Dragonflies buzzed about, telling me there was water nearby and that this world shared at least one of its creatures with our own world.

"It's… it's actually quite nice here," Caroline said, breathing in deep.

Daisy nodded. "This is incredible," she whispered.

"It is," I agreed, but there was an iron undertone to the air that reminded me it was a strange and magical place; we needed to remain on our guard. "Alright," I said, pointing at a narrow trail leading into the trees. "Let's do a little scouting. We'll follow the trail. Let's keep our eyes open."

The girls gave me firm nods, and we started

walking. Our footsteps were quiet on the forest floor. Cool, fresh air filled my lungs. Trees swayed gently. The trail beckoned us forward.

"What do you think we'll find?" Daisy asked.

"No idea," I replied. "But we need to be ready for anything."

We followed the narrow trail deeper into the forest. Trees surrounded us on all sides, their branches reaching high into the sky. The air felt cool and fresh against my skin. It smelled of pine and earth. The trail looked well-used in the past, with worn dirt and flattened grass. But at the edges, it was beginning to lose its battle with the wild growth. It hadn't been used for some time.

As we walked, my eyes kept drifting to patches of iron ore scattered on the ground. They glinted in the sunlight that filtered through the leaves. It reminded me of the untapped resources this new world held. Imagine just being able to mine it from the surface like this. It once again reminded me of what would happen if word of this magic came out – people would rush to strip this place. Who knew what other precious metals could be found here?

Daisy walked beside me, holding her new Remington 870 shotgun. Caroline followed close behind us. Her eyes darted around, taking in our surroundings with scholarly interest.

As we walked, the forest was quiet except for leaves rustling and birds calling in the distance. The birdsong sounded familiar, which meant that the birds from our own world prospered here as well. All in all, the worlds had to be connected in some way for wildlife to be so similar. Or maybe one world was just a magical extension of the other?

"Sean, do you think there are people here?" Daisy asked, rousing me from my thoughts. She spoke softly, almost whispering.

I shook my head. "I don't know. We need to be careful. We have no idea what kind of dangers might be waiting for us. This could be the world that the goblins and the trolls came from."

"You're right," Caroline said. "I hope it isn't, though. I wouldn't want to face a troll…"

I grinned and nodded in agreement as we kept walking. The soft ground muffled our footsteps.

Gradually, the trees began to thin out. I spotted the first signs that people had been here before. An old wooden fence stuck out of the undergrowth. A broken cart wheel lay abandoned by the trail.

I pointed to the remnants. "Look at that. We might be getting close to something."

Daisy's eyes widened. "Do you think it's a village?"

"Could be," I said. "Let's keep going and find out."

We continued down the trail. Soon, we saw what appeared to be buildings through the trees, and the trail opened up into a large clearing. A village stood before us — little more than a cluster of one and two-story buildings made of wood, stone, and clay. They looked old, like something from medieval times, and most of them were dilapidated and showed signs of abandonment. Roofs sagged, some walls had crumbled, and weeds were beginning to reclaim the paths while vines crawled up the walls.

The village was silent. No people moved between the buildings. No smoke rose from chimneys. A heavy feeling hung in the air.

"Looks abandoned," I said softly, keeping my shotgun in a low-ready position as I scanned the village from behind a tree trunk, wanting to remain unseen while we scoped out the place.

"Yeah," Daisy agreed from her position.

We waited a little longer to see if there was anything alive. As we stood there, we noticed signs of destruction deeper into the village. Some of the buildings had collapsed. Others had burn marks and holes in their walls.

"This place looks like it was attacked," Caroline whispered.

"But by what?" Daisy asked. She gripped her shotgun tighter.

I scanned the village carefully. "Let's take a closer look. See what we can see."

We approached the first building slowly. It was a small house with a caved-in roof. The door hung loosely, barely attached, and all the windows were broken. We stacked up on the door as discussed, and I swept in first, moving right while Daisy buttonhooked in behind me and swept left. Together, we covered all corners while keeping our exposure to the fatal funnel of the doorway limited.

The floor groaned under my feet as I took position. The room was clear, and broken furniture and debris covered the floor. The next two rooms were empty as well, and Daisy and I emerged together after our sweep. "No one's been here for a while," I said to Caroline.

"What do you think happened here?" Daisy asked.

I shrugged. "I'm not sure. But whatever it was, it left this place in ruins."

We walked through the rest of the village. Every building showed signs of damage. Walls had crumbled. Roofs were torn apart. It looked like something huge had rampaged through, destroying everything. We cleared the larger buildings that were still largely intact, but we stuck to peeking through windows and doorways for the ones that had been damaged. It'd be a particularly disappointing end to our adventuring careers if a random collapsing building ended it all for us.

The silence felt heavy as we walked. No voices.

No movement. The village seemed completely abandoned.

Or so it seemed.

As we rounded a corner where the village hugged the forest, I discerned a small shelter made of wood scraps and cloth. For a moment, I thought the person sitting out in front of it was a corpse, propped up to appear sitting by some twisted psychopath, but she opened her rheumy eyes at us when we stepped forward, and she seemed not at all surprised to see us. Her hair was gray, and her skin looked weathered.

She remained seated. I gave a quick nod to Daisy to keep an eye on our surroundings, fearing some kind of ambush, as I cautiously moved up. I didn't aim my shotgun at her directly, but I held it ready so a quick movement would line up the sights and allow me to squeeze off a slug if I needed to.

"Greetings," she croaked in a weak voice. "Who are you?"

I tried to sound friendly, but I must have appeared shifty as my eyes kept darting back and forth. "We're travelers," I said. "We're not here to hurt you. Can you tell us what happened here?"

The old woman hesitated. She remained extremely calm as she sat there in lotus position. As I watched her, I realized there was something unreal — something otherworldly about her. I couldn't exactly place it, but the way she sat there — well, she seemed almost unnatural.

"My name is Greida," she said, avoiding my question for now. "Who are you?" she simply asked again.

Apparently, she needed names. "I'm Sean," I said. "These are Daisy and Caroline. What is this place? It looks like it was hit hard by someone — or something."

She nodded slowly — an extremely controlled motion free of any shakes or stirs. "This village is called Harrwick. Or it *was* called Harrwick when there were still souls here, growing crops, raising cattle, and going through the calm motions of their lives." She shrugged, the rest of her body remaining oddly motionless. "Now, it no longer needs a name."

"What happened?" Caroline asked.

The old woman turned her rheumy eyes to

Caroline. "Harrwick was attacked by a terrible creature. It came out of nowhere and destroyed everything. I'm the only one left."

"A creature?" Caroline asked. "What kind of creature?"

Greida narrowed her eyes. "Why do you wish to know?"

Caroline stepped closer to the shelter. "We want to help."

"Please tell us what you know about the creature, Greida," I put in. I tried to keep my voice calm. I didn't want to scare her, but I also wanted to remain cautious. Something about her was off — magical.

Greida's eyes moved between Daisy, Caroline, and me. "The creature... it came at night," she said. "It was huge, covered in fur, with eyes that glowed like embers in the dark."

"A troll," I muttered, noting the resemblance with what I had seen a few nights ago near my house.

The old woman's eyes, though cloudy, fixed on me with an unsettling intensity. Her gaze felt like it could pierce through my very soul. "A troll," she confirmed, nodding slightly. "It lives in a cave not far from here."

I shifted my weight, the soft ground beneath my feet sinking slightly. The air felt heavy all of a sudden — the idea that this had once been a bright and living village, all brought to an end by a troll, didn't sit right with me.

"How did it get here?" I asked.

Greida's lips tightened. "It came out of nowhere one night, driven by a hunger for destruction."

Daisy's grip on her Remington 870 tightened. She was still keeping an eye on our surroundings as I had asked her, which was good of her — she kept a level head, and that was exactly what was needed for quests like these.

"How, uh, how big is this troll?" Caroline asked, her voice barely above a whisper.

Greida turned her gaze to Caroline. The old woman's face remained unnaturally still as she spoke. "Huge. Taller than the tallest man. Its strength is beyond anything you can imagine. It destroyed our homes with ease — the way you or I would flick aside a stack of pebbles."

I glanced around at the ruins surrounding us.

Broken beams jutted from collapsed roofs. Shattered glass glinted in the sunlight. The destruction was extensive.

Caroline stepped forward, her boots crunching on the debris-strewn ground. "Why are you still here, Greida? Why didn't you leave?"

The old woman sighed. Her body remained oddly motionless. "I am bound to this village by magic. I cannot rest until the village has been avenged. But I am powerless against the troll."

My ears perked up at the mention of magic. "Bound by magic? How does that work?"

Greida's expression turned somber. The lines on her face deepened. "A long time ago, I cast a protective spell over Harrwick and became its guardian. Witches often find a village to protect. But my protective wards were not enough to stop the troll. When the troll attacked, the spell backfired and bound me here. My spirit cannot rest until the troll is destroyed."

I exchanged glances with Daisy and Caroline. They both nodded, urging me to continue.

"Greida," I said, "can we help?"

She leaned forward slightly. Her movement was

slow and deliberate. "If you truly wish to help, then I would ask you to kill the troll. But that is something I cannot ask lightly of anyone." Then, she narrowed her eyes for a moment as she studied me. "But then again, I sense you are no mere mortal… No… You hold power over the Sigils as well, do you not?"

I stepped forward, my excitement getting the better of me. "The Sigils? You know about them?"

She allowed herself a wry smile as she nodded. "Yes. My magic relies on them as well. If you slay that troll for me and grant me peace, I will transfer some of my innate powers to you. My abilities will help you master your Sigil Magic and understand it better."

Caroline stepped closer. Her eyes widened with curiosity. "What kind of abilities are those?"

Greida's eyes sparkled. A hint of hope crept into her voice. "My skill with Sigil Magic is innate." Her gaze darted to me. "Sean's skill is acquired from a book. I can make it so that he surpasses his current level, enhancing his talent and making him a natural like myself."

My heart was thumping fast. If this was true

and not some kind of trick, then it could mean a serious increase in my magical skills. While a troll was a formidable foe, it was certainly worth considering accepting Greida's mission.

Daisy turned to me. Her jaw was set, determination written across her face. "Sean, we need to do this. We can't just leave her here."

I nodded, feeling the weight of their trust. They were right, of course. Aside from ulterior motives regarding an increase in my powers, Greida's situation itself was sad, and if we could help her, we should.

The only issue was that I was unsure if we could trust her. After all, she could be anything. But then again, she seemed genuine in her request, and if she had seemed off before to me, that was likely due to her being bound by magic to this village.

I gave a firm nod, deciding to take the risk. "We'll help you, Greida. But we need more information about the troll and its lair."

Greida nodded slowly. "The cave is to the north of the village, hidden among the hills. The troll only leaves its lair at night. During the day, it sleeps."

I ran a hand through my hair, thinking. The cool air brushed against my skin. "Alright. We can't confront it directly. It's too dangerous. We'll need to use traps — lure it somehow and make short work of it without giving it a chance to attack us."

Caroline's eyes lit up. She snapped her fingers. "You can use your Wood and Metal Sigils to create traps. There's plenty of old wood and metal in the village."

I nodded. "I was thinking the same thing."

Daisy nodded eagerly. "We can gather materials and set everything up before nightfall."

I looked at Greida. Her face had softened. A faint smile played on her lips. "Thank you," she said. "Your bravery and kindness mean more to me than you know."

Either she was the world's best actress or her gratitude was genuine, and I was leaning toward the latter. I gave her a nod before turning to the girls. "Let's get to planning," I said. "We have a troll to kill."

Chapter 6

The village lay silent around us as we convened. Broken buildings and scattered debris stretched as far as the eye could see, and it saddened me to know that a troll had caused all of this terrible destruction. But a cool breeze rustled through the trees, and there was a kind of justice in thinking that we would at least try to set things right and avenge Greida and the villagers.

"So," I began, looking at each of my women in turn, "we need to set traps for the troll. As far as I can assess, taking it on directly is too risky. This creature is big and nasty, and it looks like the type of thing that might just shrug off a few slugs. And that's not something we want to find out while fighting. So, we need traps. Things that spring when it moves and that allow us to study the results from a distance without being seen so we can fall back, regroup, and make a new plan if it doesn't work."

"Yes!" Caroline agreed, seemingly impressed by my assessment and suggestion to manage the risk of this encounter. "That sounds smart."

Daisy nodded, her blonde hair swaying slightly. "What kind of traps are you thinking?"

I glanced around at the ruined structures. "We'll use my Wood and Metal Sigils to create pitfalls, spike traps, and snares. I want metal and spikes raining down on this creature and killing it. I don't want to get up close."

"There's plenty of material here," Caroline observed, eyeing the scattered wooden beams and rusty metal scraps.

I turned to her. "Caroline, could you talk to Greida? See if she has any more information about trolls that might help us. The most important thing to learn is about where we set the traps. So we need to find out what the creature's routine is — if it has any. Where is the most nearby water source? Where does it go to eat? How does it leave and enter its lair? And then, of course, any knowledge about the troll itself — weaknesses, strengths, magical stuff we might not know that might be very self-evident to a resident of this world… Really pick her brain. And while you do that, Daisy and I will get to work gathering what materials we can find."

"You got it, Sean!" she replied, heading towards the old woman's shelter.

I faced Daisy. "Let's start gathering wood. We need sturdy pieces for the traps."

We split up, combing through the village ruins. I lifted fallen beams and pulled planks from collapsed walls. Daisy worked nearby, her movements quick and efficient. We piled our findings in the village center, creating a substantial heap of wood and metal. We focused on small pieces that would be easy to transport — after all, my magic could meld it all together, and we could transport it in a wheelbarrow like this.

And making a wheelbarrow was pretty simple…

I summoned the Sigil book, feeling the familiar surge of energy. Focusing on the Wood and Metal Sigils, I channeled its power into the gathered materials. The wood transformed before our eyes, knitting back together and becoming solid and strong. I used my magic to shape it into a wheelbarrow. Wooden wheels would not be ideal in all circumstances, but there were three of us to push and pull it.

Daisy whistled. "That never gets old," she said, running her hand along the surface of the wheelbarrow after I finished work on it.

I shot her a grin, and we began loading up the pieces of wood, rusted tools, cart wheels, and other scraps. As we worked, I kept scanning our surroundings. The village remained quiet, but I couldn't shake the feeling of dread that emanated from this place. And it made sense, of course — at night, the troll would wake up and lay waste to its surroundings. Its presence pressed on the land even during the day.

About half an hour passed, and our pile of materials had grown considerably when Caroline returned from her talk with Greida.

I wiped the sweat from my forehead and smiled at her. "Found out anything?"

"Well, she repeated that the troll sleeps during the day," she reported. "It only comes out at night. She also told me it's extra vulnerable to fire and acid, and that its wounds heal relatively quickly if not caused by fire or acid."

"Hmm," I hummed. "Well, we don't have acid, but we could set fire to a pit if it falls in. That should be doable."

She nodded. "Setting the creature on fire would be the best. Also, she said it drinks water likely from a nearby creek, and that there is only one entrance to its cave. Finally, it has to hunt for its food, but it can really glut and then not eat for several days — weeks even — so it doesn't hunt every night."

"Alright," I said, processing the information.

This was useful, at least. "Anything else?"

"Not really," Caroline said. "The poor woman just seems devastated that she has lost her charge but hopeful that we have offered to help her out."

I nodded. "Well, here's hoping we can actually help her out. We should use the daylight to set up the traps. We should scout its lair and build them just outside where it leaves and heads over to the creek — that will be the funnel we can catch it in. If we can get it stuck in some kind of pit and then set fire to it, that would be perfect. Ideally, we won't have to fire a single round, and the troll will never even see us."

Daisy wiped sweat from her forehead with the back of her hand. "Where's the lair?"

I pointed north. "Greida said it's hidden in the hills that way. We should head out soon to give ourselves enough time."

Caroline and Daisy exchanged glances, then nodded in agreement.

"Let's get moving," Caroline said, adjusting her backpack.

I checked my shotgun one last time, making sure it was loaded. "Stay alert," I warned. "We don't know what else might be out there."

With our weapons ready and our wheelbarrow full of materials, we set out towards the northern hills. The ruined village fell away behind us as we entered the dense forest, the sound of our footsteps muffled by the thick carpet of leaves and pine needles.

Chapter 7

We pushed through the dense forest, heading north toward the hills. Greida had told us the troll's lair was hidden there. The sun peeked through the leaves above us, creating patches of light on the ground. Birds chirped, and leaves rustled in the cool air. Our footsteps were quiet on the thick layer of leaves and pine needles. The wheelbarrow we'd packed with trap materials squeaked as we maneuvered it over the uneven ground.

I kept my shotgun ready, constantly looking around for danger. Daisy and Caroline walked beside me, their eyes alert and weapons prepared, with Caroline on wheelbarrow duty. The forest was eerily quiet, but we pressed on, determined to find the troll's lair and set our traps before dark.

After about an hour of walking, we reached the base of the hills. The ground became steeper, and the path narrowed. We had to move carefully to avoid slipping on loose rocks and dirt. The trees thinned out, and I heard the sound of running water nearby.

"There's the creek," I said, pointing toward the sound. "The troll probably drinks from there. Its lair should be close."

Daisy nodded. "Let's keep going. We need to find that cave."

We followed the creek's sound and soon spotted a cave entrance hidden among the rocks. The opening was large and dark and directly under a rock outcropping, which would be perfect for what I had in mind. I motioned for Daisy and Caroline to stay back as I approached carefully, my shotgun raised.

"Wait here and watch our backs," I whispered to them. "I'll check it out."

They nodded, scanning the area for any movement. I took a deep breath and stepped closer to the cave entrance, peering inside. It was almost pitch black, but I could make out rough stone walls and a narrow passage leading deeper into the hill. A loud rumbling came from deep within, and it took me a moment to place it. But then, I realized.

Snoring…

The thing was snoring.

I backed away and rejoined Daisy and Caroline. "It's definitely the troll's lair," I said quietly. "And it's definitely asleep. Time to set up the traps."

We unloaded the materials from the wheelbarrow and got to work. I used the Wood and Metal Sigils to shape the wood and metal into trap components. The power flowed through me, transforming the materials before our eyes.

"We'll start with the pit trap," I said, marking an

area just outside the cave entrance. It was an area the troll would have to step in. "If we can get the troll to fall in, we'll have a chance to finish it off."

Daisy and Caroline helped me dig a deep pit using the shovels I made with my Sigil Magic. A big blessing was that the ground was very soft but moist, letting us dig deep and fast. The only obstacles were roots, but roots were wood, and my Sigil Magic made short work of them. We worked fast, knowing we had to finish before nightfall. As we dug, I used the Wood Sigil to reinforce the pit's sides with planks I wrought.

Once it was deep enough, I used the Metal Sigil to create a lid with a spiked top. It was designed for us to lower from the rock outcropping with ropes, dropping it down if the troll stepped out of the cave and fell into the pit. The metal bars were strong and sharp, and I hoped they'd hold the creature if we caught it.

Next, we lined the bottom of the pit with flammable materials — dry leaves and twigs and stick were the best things we could find. While Daisy and I made a nice flammable bed, Caroline already got a fire going on top of the rock outcropping. The troll wouldn't see it or smell it, since Caroline was very skilled at making a good fire.

When Daisy and I had lined the bottom with flammable materials, we still had some daylight left. And that was good because we still needed to cover the pit. I looked around and smiled at Daisy, who was sweating from all the work. "Let's use branches and leaves to hide it."

She nodded and began gathering branches and leaves while I used the magic of my Wood Sigil to create a sturdy framework for the covering. We laid the branches and leaves over the pit, making sure it blended in with the forest floor.

"That should do it," I said, stepping back. "Now we need to set up more traps around the area, in case the pit doesn't work."

We spent the next hour setting up additional traps near the cave entrance. I used the Sigils to create snares and spike traps, placing them strategically to catch the troll if it tried to escape or find us, buying us enough time to fall back and regroup. Daisy and Caroline helped me position everything, making sure it was all hidden and ready. When that was done, they focused on the finishing touches while I meditated to recover my mana.

As we finished, the sun began to set, casting long shadows across the forest. The air grew colder, and the forest sounds changed as night approached. An eerie stillness seemed to settle on the forest, as if all creatures were preparing for the troll to awaken.

"We should head to the top of the outcropping," I said, looking around. "We need to drop the cage on it if it falls into the pit."

"Don't you think it'll get suspicious?" Daisy asked. "The pit might be covered but… the terrain looks kinda different."

"That's why *I* will be down there," I said. "If it doesn't fall for it, I'll hop out and fire at it. With any luck, it'll get angry and charge, dropping into the pit anyway. At least, it will if it's a little stupid."

"That's an awful big risk," Caroline muttered.

"Which is why we have the other traps," I said. "If it doesn't fall for it and chooses to chase me, I will lead it through the funnel, and it will get slowed down. We'll regroup on the outcropping and fall back to the village. If necessary, we can head through the portal home and close it."

Caroline thought for a moment, then nodded. "Alright, it sounds like you have all bases covered."

"And if it falls in, we drop flaming branches in the pit?" Daisy asked, shouldering her Remington.

I grinned and nodded. "You got it."

We climbed to the top of the rock outcropping. By now, the sun had set, and the sky had turned a deep purple. Stars slowly began to appear overhead as Caroline finished her work with the fire, making sure it made no smoke and that the wind carried its scent away from the troll's cave.

I felt excited and anxious at the same time. This was dangerous, but I couldn't deny the thrill of it all.

We took our positions on the outcropping, lying low to stay hidden. From here, we could see the cave entrance and our trap clearly. I positioned myself near the ropes that would drop the spiked lid into the pit. Daisy and Caroline took positions on either side of me, each of them holding part of the rope that kept the spiked cage top in place.

"Remember," I whispered, "if it doesn't fall into the pit, I'll lure it through the other traps. Stay hidden until we see what happens."

Daisy nodded. Her eyes were focused on the cave entrance. "Got it, Sean."

"We'll be ready," Caroline said softly.

The forest around us grew darker. Nocturnal creatures began to stir, their sounds filling the air. We waited in silence, our eyes fixed on the cave entrance. My heart pounded in my chest.

Time passed slowly as we lay there. The minutes ticked by. I glanced at Daisy and Caroline. The faint moonlight illuminated their faces. They looked determined and excited. Like me, they seemed very much alive with the thrill of this hunt. I dwelled on how lucky I was to have them here with me. These extraordinary women with a lust for exploration and adventure were a perfect match, and it almost seemed as if fate had brought us together to venture out into the unknown together.

I thought about everything that had led us here.

The magic we'd discovered. The bond we'd formed. It was exhilarating to be part of something so extraordinary.

As we lay there, the forest grew quieter. The night sounds became more distant as if the critters of the forest knew the troll would be awakening soon and were leaving the vicinity in anticipation of the arrival of the forest's apex predator. We watched the cave entrance, waiting for any sign of movement. I took a deep breath to steady my nerves.

Then I heard it — a faint rustling sound from within the cave. My heart skipped a beat. Daisy and Caroline tensed beside me; their eyes locked on the cave entrance. They tightened their grip on the rope, ready to spring into action.

The rustling grew louder. I saw a shadow move within the darkness. The troll was waking up. I glanced at Daisy and Caroline and gave them a nod. They nodded back.

We waited, every muscle in our bodies ready for action. The troll's movements grew more pronounced. I could hear its heavy footsteps echoing within the cave.

As the troll lumbered closer to the entrance, I felt a surge of adrenaline. This was it — the moment we had been preparing for.

The earth shook as the creature stirred within its cave, and then a mighty roar came from the cave — as if the creature was announcing its arrival to everything out there, to all the creatures it considered prey. The roar spoke of death and destruction, and I understood why the creatures of the forest had left. The silence that followed that roar was almost as deafening as the roar itself.

I exchanged a look with my women, giving them a steadying nod as we got ready. Daisy and I had our shotguns lying on the ground beside us, and we were ready to jump into action the moment it was needed as we peered over the edge of the outcropping.

Then, it came.

The troll's massive form lumbered from the cave. It had to stoop to exit, and it stretched and peered into the darkness, its glowing eyes scanning the area. It took a step forward, then another. Its heavy footsteps shook the ground. My heart raced as I watched, waiting for the creature to step into the trap.

"Steady," I whispered to Daisy and Caroline.

As the troll lumbered out of its cave, I felt my heart racing. Its heavy footsteps shook the ground beneath us. The creature's glowing eyes scanned the area, but it didn't notice our trap. It took another step forward, then another.

"Here it comes," I whispered to Daisy and Caroline.

We watched from our hiding spot on the outcropping as the troll approached the pit. Its massive form cast long shadows in the moonlight. The ground groaned under its weight with each step. It seemed to take its time as it loudly sniffed the air. I tightened my grip on the ropes, hoping that it wouldn't be suspect, smelling either us or the woodfire. My palms were sweaty, and I felt the nervous energy of the girls beside me.

Then, the troll growled and stepped forward. Its foot landed on the pit cover.

The ground under the troll gave way, and the apex predator of this forest let out a deafening roar as it fell into the pit, outsmarted by three humans. Its body crashed onto the spikes below.

"Now!" I hissed.

I released the ropes with all my strength, at the same time as the girls. With a clanking and turmoil like the drums of hell, the spiked lid dropped onto the troll, striking true. The spikes drove deep into the troll's hide, and its roars of agony and fury echoed through the forest. It thrashed against the spikes, but that only made it worse.

"The fire!" I shouted over the turmoil.

Caroline was on her feet in a moment, with Daisy beside her, and I covered them with the Mossberg as they tossed flaming brands from the campfire down into the pit. The troll shrieked in fear and rage as the dry leaves and twigs at the bottom of the pit caught fire. We had set everything up well, and despite the troll thrashing about, flames reared up at once with thick smoke, engulfing the creature.

"It's working," Daisy said. Her eyes were wide as she watched the fire spread in the pit. The troll thrashed about with great fury, but the lid we had dropped on it was heavy, and several of the spikes had driven deep into the earth and the remainder of the trap's wooden frame, making it difficult for the beast to get out. Given enough time, it certainly would… but its fur was starting to catch fire, and there would not be enough time.

The trap worked just like we had planned.

"I can't believe it," Daisy hummed. She gripped her shotgun tightly. Caroline watched with a look of satisfaction in her eyes.

We stayed on the outcropping, watching the fire burn. The heat was intense. Sweat beaded on my forehead. The troll's roars grew weaker. After what felt like hours, there was only the crackling of flames.

I let out a long breath. "I think it's over."

"Should we check?" Daisy asked.

I nodded. "Let's go down. We need to make sure it's really dead."

We carefully made our way down from the outcropping. The fire still burned in the pit. Thick smoke filled the air, and the scent of burning flesh was nauseating. All around us, the forest was still very silent, as if all of its inhabitants were listening with bated breath, not yet believing that the troll that had terrorized their home was really dead.

We approached cautiously. Daisy and I took the front, our shotguns ready as we aimed at the smoldering pit. Nothing stirred within except smoke, but I moved as close as I could, gesturing for the girls to hold, making sure I had the breeze at my back.

I peered into the pit and caught sight of it for a moment through the thick smoke. The troll's massive body lay still, pinned by the spikes. The fire had consumed most of its fur. Its skin was charred and blackened. It no longer moved, and even though I was upwind of the corpse, I could smell the foul stink of burning flesh, and I had to fight the need to retch.

"Is it... dead?" Caroline asked.

"Looks like it," I replied, covering my mouth. "But let's wait until the fire dies down before we get any closer."

We stood by the pit, watching the flames. The air was thick with the smell of burning flesh and wood. My stomach turned, but I forced myself to keep looking. As we kept guard, the fire slowly died, and a sense of ease returned to us. Parts of the troll became visible now, charred and destroyed.

"That was intense," Daisy said. She wiped sweat from her brow with the back of her hand.

Caroline nodded. "I'm glad we didn't have to face it directly. Look at the size of that thing."

I stepped closer to the pit's edge. The troll's body was enormous. Its bulging muscles and layers of fat were visible still — the fire simply hadn't been able to consume it all. I shuddered at the thought of facing it in combat.

"We should head back to Greida," I said. "She'll want to know it's over."

"Good idea," Daisy replied. "She'll be relieved."

"Hold on a minute," I said. "I want to take a closer look at the troll before we go."

Daisy and Caroline turned to me, their expressions curious.

"Are you sure?" Daisy asked, her grip tightening on her Remington.

I nodded. "Yeah, I think it's important we understand what we were up against. I also want to check out its lair. There might be something of value in it."

The girls exchanged a look and nodded. "Yeah, I

suppose that makes sense," Daisy said. "Let's wait a bit longer to let the smoldering die down."

We waited a while longer until there were only smoldering embers and thick smoke hanging in the air. The troll's massive form lay motionless, impaled by the spikes we had set.

I approached the edge of the pit cautiously, shining my flashlight down at the charred remains. The troll was even more imposing up close. Its fur had been burned away, revealing blackened skin stretched over enormous muscles and thick layers of fat. It also had massive claws and a powerful jaw. The creature was just one big arsenal of walking weaponry. Judging by its legs, it could be very fast if it wanted to. It was good to know this, since I still had a troll to deal with back home.

"Look at the size of those muscles," I said, moving the flashlight beam across the troll's body. "I wouldn't be surprised if this thing could just tear a human in two like we do a piece of paper."

Daisy stepped up beside me, peering down into the pit. "I'm glad we didn't have to. That thing would have ripped us to shreds."

Caroline joined us, her eyes wide as she took in the sight. "Our traps were the right call. We wouldn't have stood a chance in a direct confrontation."

I nodded, feeling a mixture of relief and pride in our accomplishment. "We did good. But let's check out the cave before we head back. There might be something valuable in there."

We moved away from the pit and approached the cave entrance once more. I swept my flashlight beam across the opening, revealing rough stone walls and a narrow passage leading deeper into the hill. The air inside was cool and damp, carrying the scent of earth and stone and the stink of the troll that had lived there for a long time.

"Stay close," I instructed, stepping into the cave. "We don't know what might be in here."

Daisy and Caroline followed close behind as we made our way down the narrow passage. Our footsteps echoed off the stone walls, the sound amplified in the confined space. I kept the flashlight moving, checking for any signs of danger or anything unusual.

After a few minutes of walking, the passage

opened up into a larger chamber. As I swept the flashlight around, the beam caught something glinting in the center of the room. My heart rate picked up as I realized what it was.

"Look at that," I said, moving closer. "Gold and silver coins."

Daisy let out a low whistle. "That could be worth a lot back on Earth."

Caroline nodded, her eyes fixed on the pile. "We should take it with us. It might come in handy."

I crouched down to examine the coins more closely. They were old and dirty, but they were real enough. Money wasn't a problem for me since my investments had paid off, but I wouldn't say no to a bit more. Me and the girls would divide it. I pulled out a pouch from my pack and began scooping the coins into it.

"This is quite a haul," I said, feeling the weight of the pouch increase. "The troll must have been collecting these for a while."

Once I had gathered all the coins, I stood up and secured the pouch in my pack. "Let's get out of here," I said. "We've got what we came for."

We made our way back through the narrow

passage to the cave entrance. The cool night air felt refreshing after the damp atmosphere of the cave. We paused for a moment to catch our breath and get our bearings.

"Well, that was something," Daisy said, running a hand through her hair.

Caroline nodded and gave a chuckle that seemed to release some of her nerves. "Honestly, I still can't believe we managed to take down a troll."

"Neither can I," I admitted with a grin. "But we did it. Now let's head back and tell Greida the good news."

We set off through the forest once more, our path illuminated by the moonlight shining through the trees and the flashlight that Caroline now held. As we moved away from the troll's lair, the air cleared, and it was a welcome change. As we walked, I found myself reflecting on everything that had happened.

"You know," I said, breaking the silence, "I never thought I'd be doing something like this when I moved to Waycross."

Daisy chuckled. "Life's full of surprises, ain't it?

I never expected I would see stuff like this either."

"That's for sure," Caroline agreed. "But it's exciting. I… I always had a feeling there was more to this world than what we could see. I'm happy we did this. I… I have a feeling our lives are about to become even more exciting."

I nodded, grateful for their presence. "I think so, too. And I'm happy to share this with you."

We continued our journey back to the village, tired but satisfied with what we had accomplished. The forest around us was quiet, save for the occasional rustle of leaves or distant animal call. It seemed the forest's inhabitants were still cautious, but I knew a semblance of normalcy would return now that the troll was dead.

Despite the darkness, I felt a sense of lightness. We had faced a great danger and emerged victorious.

Chapter 8

We returned to Harrwick under the moonlight. The village was quiet, with broken buildings and scattered debris all around. As the wind turned, I caught a whiff of the lingering scent of smoke from our battle with the troll. There was something sad about the place, but I knew we had at least avenged its inhabitants. If there were more villages in this magical world, our actions would protect them at least from this particular troll.

Greida's shelter came into view. She sat in the same spot, her posture unchanged. She still had that sad, haunting quality about her, and her eyes glinted in the moonlight as we approached. She seemed to look straight through us, and I felt a pang of uncertainty from my women as we approached the witch.

I took the lead and stepped forward. "We've done it," I told her. "The troll is dead."

Greida nodded slowly. "I sensed it, travelers. Thank you. You have avenged Harrwick. In doing so, you have set my spirit free. I am indebted to you, for you saved me from a life of haunting."

Daisy shifted her Remington. "Well, we couldn't leave you like that. It was the right thing to do."

Caroline moved closer. "What happens now, Greida?"

Greida let out a long breath. "I rest," she simply said. "Your actions have given me back my freedom. The ruins of Harrwick will fade. But who knows, in the future, some souls may find the ruined buildings and put them to new use. I do hope so, for it is good to have the land alive rather than empty."

I looked at the ruins around us, then back to Greida. "I hope so too."

We stood in silence for a moment. The weight of our accomplishment settled over us. A cool breeze rustled through the trees, carrying the scent of pine and earth. Hopefully, there would be a new beginning for Harrwick.

Finally, Greida looked at each of us. Already, her load seemed lighter, and it seemed almost as if she were becoming more... transparent. "You have done more than I could have hoped for," she said. "I am deeply grateful." Then, she turned to me. "Sean, there is one more thing. I promised you a reward — to make you more innately skilled with your Sigil Magic."

I felt a flutter of excitement in my chest as I stepped forward. "How can you do that exactly?"

Greida straightened up. "I will transfer my natural Sigil mastery to you. This will meld your Sigil Grimoire with your spirit, transforming it into a Spirit Grimoire."

"What does that mean?" Daisy asked.

"It means that Sean will be able to cast spells without the physical book," Greida explained. "The book will disappear and become part of him. It will also grant him an additional Grimoire slot for arranging Sigils." She offered a rare smile as she turned to me. "This second slot will allow you to store more Sigils and create a second arrangement of Sigils."

It sounded amazing. Having to hold the book was a bit of a burden, and if we could somehow bypass it. Well, that would be great. I glanced at Daisy and Caroline. They both nodded encouragingly.

"Are there any risks?" I asked Greida.

"No," she said. "I am fading and will no longer be of this world. But my skill is mine to transfer to a worthy soul or to let die with me. But you are worthy, Sean. It is my gift to you. You have earned it."

I took a deep breath. "Alright. Then I accept your reward with gratitude."

Greida closed her eyes. "Very well. I will perform the ritual." She straightened her posture and closed her eyes. "Sean, come closer," she said.

I stepped forward, my heart racing. Daisy and Caroline stood nearby, watching intently. The night air felt cool against my skin, and I could hear the gentle rustling of leaves in the breeze. The broken buildings of Harrwick loomed around us, dark silhouettes against the starry sky. I somehow felt the hand of fate in all this, like it was supposed to happen this way.

As I stood there, Greida began to chant in a language I didn't recognize. Her words had a rhythmic quality, rising and falling in a steady pattern. As she spoke, I felt a tingling sensation start in my fingertips. It spread up my arms and through my body, growing stronger with each passing moment. The prickling energy converged at my core, connecting with the magical might already contained within.

I glanced at Daisy and Caroline. Their eyes were wide, and they stood perfectly still, as if afraid to disrupt whatever was happening.

The tingling intensified, becoming almost painful. I clenched my jaw, trying to stay focused on Greida. Her chanting grew louder, filling the night air with a strange, resonant quality.

Suddenly, images flashed before my eyes, taking away the ruins of Harrwick and bringing to a better time. In those visions, I saw Greida as a young woman, her face bright and full of life and laughter. She stood before an old man who showed her how to cast spells, who taught her the trade. They were in a village that struck me as medieval, but it wasn't as full of trees and deposits of ore as this world was.

Had she learned her magic someplace else?

Then, the image shifted. I watched her protect the village, heal the sick, and tend to crops. She was a guardian, loved by all. It was nothing like the hated witches back on Earth – she was benevolent and good.

The images shifted again. I saw the troll's attack on Harrwick. Buildings crumbled, people screamed, and Greida fought desperately to save them. But she was no battle mage. The Sigils she had absorbed during her long tenure as the Witch of Harrwick were Sigils of healing, Sigils to strengthen crops, and Sigils to ward against evil. She tried to use those latter ones to weave a spell against the troll, but I felt her anguish as her spell backfired, trapping her spirit in the ruined village.

Energy surged through me, and Greida's chanting reached a peak. Then, abruptly, silence fell.

Greida opened her eyes, which now glowed with an inner light. "It is done," she said softly. "The Grimoire is now part of you. You no longer need to hold it to cast spells."

I took a deep breath, feeling different. The power felt more integrated, more natural. "Thank you, Greida," I said.

She smiled faintly. "You are a true master of Sigil Magic now, Sean. Use this power wisely."

I nodded, still processing what had happened. "I will."

Daisy stepped forward. "Sean, are you okay?" she asked, her eyes wide.

"I'm fine," I replied, giving her a small smile. "It's a lot to take in, but I feel stronger."

Caroline moved closer. "Greida, how will this change Sean's magic?" she asked.

Greida nodded slowly. She was fading even more, as if the ritual had cost her much of her remaining strength. The lines around her eyes deepened as she spoke. "Arranging Sigils within the Grimoire allows for more powerful combined spells. The Portal Sigil led you to Harrwick – which lies in an elemental realm of wood and metals – because it resonated in your Grimoire with Wood and Metal elements."

I nodded. Caroline had already suspected there was a relation between the destination of the portal and the other Sigils in my book, and she had been right. Still, I had more questions, and it seemed like Greida was fading away, so I wanted to learn as much as I could before she would vanish. "Resonated?" I asked. "What does that mean?"

Greida leaned forward slightly. "Each Sigil has its own elemental force. When combined, these forces can create new spells or lead to different destinations when used with the Portal Sigil. The Wood and Metal Sigils brought you here."

Caroline's eyes lit up with interest. "So, different combinations can take us to different places?"

Greida nodded. Her thin, gray hair swayed with the movement. "Exactly. The possibilities are vast. It's about understanding the synergy between the elements."

I felt a surge of curiosity. My mind raced with potential combinations. "How do I arrange the Sigils now that the book is part of me?"

Greida's eyes softened. She raised a hand, gesturing towards me. "Close your eyes, Sean. Picture the Grimoire in your mind. See the Sigils as they are arranged now."

I closed my eyes, focusing on the mental image. And sure enough, in my mind, I saw the familiar Grimoire. The Wood, Metal, and Portal Sigils glowed on the pages, just as they had in the physical book. But they were a part of me now. Below it, as Greida had promised, was a second book — a second slot for me to arrange Sigils in.

"Now," Greida said, her voice gentle, "visualize moving the Sigils. Rearrange them in your mind."

I imagined shifting the Wood Sigil next to the Metal Sigil. The energy in my mind pulsed, responding to the change. It felt like moving pieces on a game board, but the board was inside my head.

"Good," Greida said. "Feel the flow of mana. Let it guide you."

I felt the mana channels in my body responding to the new arrangement. It was like a puzzle clicking into place. The energy flowed more smoothly, adapting to the new configuration.

"Now open your eyes," Greida instructed.

I did as she said. The sensation of the Grimoire remained with me, a constant presence in the back of my mind. I knew I could call upon the magic and cast my spells if I needed to. It was inside me now — no longer something that I could only achieve with the book. "I can feel the difference," I said, amazed at the new connection I felt to the magic.

Greida smiled. Her face looked less worn now, as if sharing her knowledge had revitalized her. But she was fading still, and I knew she would soon be gone. "You've taken the first step. Experiment with different combinations. You'll discover new spells and destinations."

Daisy watched me closely. She gripped her Remington tighter. "Does it feel different?" she asked.

I nodded, trying to find the right words. "Yes, it's more... intuitive. I can sense the connections between the Sigils."

Greida sighed, drawing my attention to her. Her form began to waver, her edges blurring like a mirage in the desert. Her voice took on an otherworldly quality, echoing slightly in the night air. "There are other Sigils," she said. "You must seek them out."

I leaned forward, intrigued. "More Sigils? Where can we find them?"

Greida's eyes locked onto mine. "They are scattered across different realms. But be warned: dark forces are always looking for them."

A chill ran down my spine, and I tightened my grip on my shotgun. "Dark forces? What kind of dark forces?"

"Powerful beings from other realms," Greida explained. Her form flickered like a candle in the wind. "They seek the Sigils to dominate and control. They will stop at nothing to obtain them."

Daisy shifted her weight, her Remington held close. "So, we're not the only ones after these Sigils?"

Greida nodded, her movement slow and deliberate. "Yes. You must be vigilant. Prepare yourselves for future challenges."

I glanced at the ruins of Harrwick surrounding us. I did not want Waycross to end up like this. I would protect my loved ones. "How do we prepare?"

"Fortify your home," Greida said. "Make it a place of strength. Deepen your studies." She shook her head as a wry smile appeared on her lips. "Do not make the mistake that I did. Do not assume you will be allowed to live safely in peace."

Caroline stepped closer, her eyes wide with curiosity. "How do we fortify our home? What should we do?"

Greida's form flickered again, growing fainter. "Use your knowledge of Sigil Magic. Build barriers, set wards. The stronger your defenses, the safer you'll be."

I nodded. "We will. We'll make our home as secure as possible." We would enjoy the times of peace we would have, but Greida was right; we should not become complacent. We would keep our guards up. Always.

"Good," Greida said, her voice growing softer.

"Remember, the Sigils hold great power. Use them wisely."

Daisy nodded firmly. "We will. Thank you, Greida. You've given us a lot to think about."

Greida's form grew even fainter, almost transparent in the moonlight. "There's one last thing," she whispered. "Trust in each other. Your bond will be your greatest strength. I thought I could do it all alone... but I was wrong. No one can do it on their own."

Caroline's eyes glistened in the dim light. "We will."

A faint smile played on Greida's lips. "Go now. Prepare. And remember, the Sigils are your path to power and protection."

I took a deep breath, feeling the weight of her words settle over me. "We will. We'll be ready for whatever comes."

Greida's form began to dissipate, her edges blurring into the night air. "Thank you, travelers. You've given me peace."

With those final words, Greida's form dissolved completely, fading into the night air. The energy around us shifted, feeling lighter. The oppressive weight that had hung over the village lifted, leaving behind a sense of peace. Still, we all felt a spark of sadness at Greida's fate.

We would honor her by heeding her warning.

I looked at Daisy and Caroline, taking in their expressions. They seemed sad as well, but when they returned my look, hope and excitement blazed in their eyes, and I offered them both a grin. "Let's head back," I said. "Looks like we've got a lot of work to do."

Daisy smiled, shouldering her Remington. "Agreed," she said as Caroline took a deep breath, her eyes scanning the ruins of Harrwick one last time before she nodded at me.

We gathered our supplies, checking our weapons and packs. The ruined buildings of Harrwick stood silent around us as we returned through the forest toward the portal that would take us home. The path back through the forest felt different now, less threatening, and that was a good thing; it was dark, and we were tired. Next time, I would bring a tent...

As we walked, the cool night air brushed against my skin. The sound of our footsteps on the forest floor and the occasional rustle of leaves filled the silence. The weight of Greida's words hung over us, a reminder of the challenges that lay ahead.

Chapter 9

I stepped through the portal first, and the familiar sight of my living room materialized before me. The warm glow of the lamp cast soft shadows on the wooden paneling. The old couch, with its worn leather upholstery, stood invitingly in the center of the room. I let out a long breath, feeling the tension in my muscles ease.

It was good to be back.

Daisy came through right behind me, her Remington clutched tightly in her hands. She looked around, her eyes wide. "We're back," she said, her voice barely above a whisper. She set her shotgun against the wall and stretched her arms above her head as she chuckled. "That might have been the most exciting time in all of my life!"

Caroline stepped through, and I closed the portal behind her. She nodded, her gaze sweeping across the room as she sighed, happy to be home as well. She turned to me, her eyes bright. "And Sean, your new abilities... they're incredible."

I smiled, feeling a surge of pride. "Thanks. It seems like we're at the start of an interesting journey." I chuckled as I set my Mossberg down next to Daisy's Remington and walked over to the kitchen table. "We have a lot to think about and prepare for."

I placed my rucksack on the table and pulled out the pouch of coins we'd found in the troll's lair. "And a nice reward for us all. It's always good to have some gold and silver to fall back on in hard times, right? Let's divvy these up!"

Daisy clapped her hands and smiled, and I handed her the pouch with a grin. "Let's count 'em," she said, pouring the coins onto the table. They clattered against the wood, a mix of gold and silver glinting in the lamplight.

Caroline joined us, leaning in to examine the coins. "These look old," she said, picking one up and turning it over in her hand. "But there is nothing stamped on them."

"Who knows what world they came from?" I asked, watching as they began sorting through the pile. "We'll need to find a safe place for them. But right now, we should focus on what we learned and what to do next." I pulled out a chair and sat down at the kitchen table, feeling the weight of exhaustion settling over me. It had been a very long day. Somehow, it was still evening here — not night as it had been in Harrwick.

Daisy looked up from the coins, her expression serious. "I'm thinking we need to fortify the house, like Greida said. Make it stronger." She glanced around the room, her gaze lingering on the windows and doors. "With your abilities, Sean, we can create some sturdy defenses."

"You're right," Caroline agreed. She turned to me, her eyes bright with excitement. "And we need to experiment with the new Sigil combinations. There's so much to learn about what they can do."

I took a deep breath, considering their words. "You both make good points. We have a lot of work ahead of us. But for now, let's get some rest. We can start fresh in the morning. I think you girls should stay here tonight, and not just because I enjoy it, but we might have drawn the attention of something, and I want you here where I can protect you."

Daisy grinned. "Sure," she hummed teasingly. "To *protect* us, right?" She gave Caroline a playful poke, and she covered her mouth and giggled.

I grinned. "Well, there might be some ulterior motives involved, but still… it's the safest."

Daisy winked at me. "Never gonna say no to that."

"Same here," Caroline hummed.

I grinned and nodded. "Alright, but first, let's make sure the house is secure for the night." I stood up and walked to the front door, checking the locks, then set the alarm in place.

Caroline and Daisy moved to the windows. They pulled the curtains closed and tested the latches, making sure the strong bolts I had made were all in place.

When we had checked the whole place, the three of us headed into the living room with a pot of freshly brewed tea. I sat down on the couch, feeling it give under my weight as I sank down.

Daisy joined me on one side, her shoulder brushing against mine. "You know," she said, "there's a lot of scrap iron and wood back in Harrwick. We could use that for future projects."

Caroline, who sat down on my other side, nodded enthusiastically. "That's a great idea. We could use the portal to bring it here." She looked at me, waiting for my reaction.

"It's a good plan," I agreed. "We'll need those materials to build up the defenses, and I can work well with wood and iron."

Daisy leaned back, her eyes closing. "I can't wait to see what we can do with all those materials. We're going to turn this place into a real fortress."

As we relaxed and recovered in the living room, the pot of tea steaming on the table, I decided it was time to practice with my new abilities. I needed to get a handle on my new Spirit Grimoire and see what I could do without the physical book.

"Alright," I said, standing up. "Time to see what this new power can do."

Daisy and Caroline looked up at me.

"You're going to practice *now*?" Caroline asked.

"Yeah," I replied. "Better to get a feel for it sooner rather than later. Plus, I'm too excited to wait."

Caroline chuckled, and Daisy joined in. "You never stop, do you?" Daisy joked.

I shot her a wink before I walked over to a small wooden table in the corner of the room. I closed my eyes and pictured the Grimoire in my mind. The Sigils were there, glowing softly. I focused on the Wood Sigil, feeling the mana flow through me.

Easy as that, I reshaped the table, repairing a few scratches and making the legs curve outward a little for style. A warm sensation spread from my hands into the wood as the effect I desired manifested.

"Look at that," Daisy said. She leaned forward on the couch, her eyes wide.

Caroline stood up and walked over to examine the table. She ran her hand along the leg, pressing down on it to test its strength. "It's perfect," she said.

I grinned. "Let's try something with metal next."

With a smile on my lips and the girls in tow, I headed into the kitchen and began removing and replacing nails and hinges, pulling them out and driving them back into the wood through my magic alone. If anything, practicing Sigil Magic in this way was even more enjoyable. It was now really something that *I* could do, and I needed nothing material to help do it.

Daisy clapped her hands as she watched the results of my magical work. "That's amazing, Sean. You're really getting the hang of this."

Caroline nodded. "You're doing great. Now, what about the Portal Sigil? Can you try rearranging the Sigils in your mind?"

"Let's see," I said, closing my eyes once more. I visualized the Grimoire and saw the three Sigils glowing on the pages. I imagined moving the Portal Sigil to the second slot, alongside the Wood Sigil, keeping the Metal Sigil alone in the first slot. The energy shifted, responding to the new arrangement.

I opened my eyes and focused on the center of the room. A faint light appeared, growing brighter. Mana blazed in my channels as I opened another portal, and Caroline and Daisy stood back, eyes wide, as I cast my spell. I felt my mana bleeding away as the spell took effect, and a portal began to form, shimmering in the air. Through it, I saw a dense forest, similar to the one we had just visited but with different trees and plants. The trees were taller, with broader leaves, and the undergrowth was thicker. And there were no deposits of metal.

"That's a forest," Daisy said. She stood up and walked closer to the portal, peering through. "It looks different from the one in Harrwick. The trees are huge!"

Caroline joined her, examining the view through the portal. "It's incredible. Can you try the Portal Sigil with the Metal Sigil next?"

I nodded and closed the portal. I took a moment to meditate to recover my mana. Then, when I felt I had enough, I closed my eyes again, rearranging the Sigils in my mind. This time, I placed the Portal Sigil alongside the Metal Sigil. The energy shifted once more, and I felt a different kind of resonance.

I opened my eyes and focused on the center of the room. A new portal formed. Through it, I saw an underground cave, its walls glistening with veins of metal. The cave seemed to stretch on endlessly, filled with rich mineral deposits. The air shimmered with heat, and I could see pools of molten metal in the distance.

I knew right away that industrialists would *kill* for this.

"An underground realm," Caroline said. She leaned closer to the portal, her eyes wide. "Look at all that metal. There are entire rivers of it!"

Daisy stepped up beside her, her mouth agape. "Imagine what we could do with all that material. We could build anything!"

I closed the portal and took a deep breath. The new abilities were incredible, but they were also draining. My head felt heavy, and I could feel sweat beading on my forehead.

"You okay, Sean?" Daisy asked, an eyebrow raised in concern.

I smiled and nodded. "It's a little taxing, so this is enough experimentation for now."

"Of course," Caroline said, and Daisy nodded, too. "Don't overexert yourself."

I sat down on the couch again and took a deep breath, feeling the excitement from testing my new abilities still coursing through me. "Let's talk about our next steps," I said. "The battles with the goblins, the undead, and the troll have shown us what we're up against. I think it's time we take the fight to the goblins in the forest. They've been attacking us, and we need to put an end to it. We're armed, we have some experience; I think we could do it."

Daisy nodded vigorously. "I reckon you're right, Sean. We've handled everything so far. We can take on those goblins too."

Caroline leaned forward, her brow furrowed. "I'm not sure," she hummed, showing her cautious side again. "We can try, but we need to be careful. The forest is their territory, and they know it better than we do. We should gather as much information as possible before we go in."

She wasn't wrong. We defeated the troll because we were careful, made a plan, and set our traps. We would have to deal with the goblins in the same way. They were weaker but more numerous. We'd need to know the terrain and act with all due care.

"You're right," I said, rubbing my chin. "We need to be smart about this. You know what? Harper knows the woods very well. He might be able to help us find the goblins' lair."

"That's a good idea," Caroline said. She sat up straighter. "Harper has lived in these woods all his life, and he goes out *a lot*. He knows every inch of them. If anyone can help us, it's him."

Daisy chimed in, "We should talk to him first thing in the mornin'. Get his advice and see if he can guide us."

I nodded. "We'll head over to Harper's place in the morning. We'll see if he's on board. But for now, my stomach is rumbling. We haven't eaten in way too long."

At that, the girls exchanged a glance before they broke out laughing. "Oh my," Caroline hummed. "I hadn't even *thought* of food… But now that you mention it!"

"Same here!" Daisy said. "Very unlike me, if I'm honest."

Laughing, I rose and beckoned them to come along. "Come on," I said. "Let's see what we can find in the kitchen!"

Chapter 10

Together, the girls and I stepped into the kitchen. I got the old stove going while the girls gathered up ingredients so we could make whatever we could make. Soon enough, the old stove radiated warmth, and we were in its cozy light. I moved to the counter and began slicing vegetables while Daisy and Caroline worked on the other side, their conversation animated and enthusiastic.

Daisy looked up from her task. "Pass me those potatoes, will you, Sean?"

I handed her the bowl of potatoes. "Here you go. What are we making tonight?"

Caroline stirred a pot on the stove. "How about a good mishmash stew of just about everything you got? We got potatoes, vegetables, some meat. Just gonna throw it all in a pan and see what happens."

"Sounds perfect," I said, adding the sliced vegetables to a large bowl. "Easy cooking. I love it."

Daisy started peeling the potatoes, her movements quick and precise. "You know, Sean, I've been thinking about what you said earlier. Taking the fight to the goblins. I'm all in for that. Wouldn't it be great if we could just hand it to them little bastards?"

Caroline nodded, adding some spices to the pot. "Me too. We've faced so much already, and I feel more alive than ever. There's no way I'm backing down now."

I felt a surge of excitement. "I'm glad to hear

that. I was hoping you'd both be up for more adventures. There's so much out there to discover."

"Absolutely," Daisy said. "Today's just the beginnin', and I wanna see what else is out there! Who knows what other worlds we might find?"

Caroline stirred the pot, the aroma of the stew filling the kitchen. "And think of all the knowledge we can gain. Every new place we visit, every creature we encounter, it's all a learning experience. I can't wait."

We continued preparing the meal, the conversation carried on. Daisy mashed the potatoes while Caroline added the final ingredients to the stew. I set the table, placing bowls and spoons neatly in place.

As the stew simmered on the stove, I looked around the kitchen. "You know, this is exactly what I envisioned when I moved here. Living a life of adventure, discovering new things, and sharing it all with some people who are worth it."

Daisy smiled. "Ain't you a sweet one?" she hummed.

Caroline smiled and lightly touched my

forearm. "It's been the adventure of a lifetime so far."

I leaned against the counter and crossed my arms. "So, tomorrow we talk to Harper, get his help with the goblins. After that, who knows?"

Daisy laughed. "I'm ready for anything. Bring it on."

I grinned broadly; her optimism was infectious. She was right — so long as we took care, there were no limits to what we could do.

The kitchen filled with the sounds of our laughter and conversation as we finished preparing dinner. We sat down at the table, bowls of steaming stew in front of us, and dug in with enthusiasm.

As we ate, we shared stories of the day's events. Daisy recounted her experience with the troll, gesturing wildly with her spoon. Caroline chimed in with her observations about the magical world we'd visited. I listened, enjoying their excitement and adding my own thoughts about the new abilities I'd gained. After, the subject shifted to old man Harper.

"He knows the forest unlike anyone else,"

Caroline said, and I noticed her uhs and ahs and stuttering were getting a lot less in present company. That made me smile because it was a good sign; she was comfortable with us.

"Agreed," I said. "We need him for this venture."

"Right," Daisy agreed. "What's the plan for talking to him tomorrow?"

I set down my spoon. "I figure we'll head over to his place first thing in the morning. We'll explain the situation and see if he can guide us through the forest. He knows some things about Waycross are odd, so he wouldn't be too surprised knowing we wanted to take out goblins. He might even find it intriguing."

Caroline took a sip of water. "Do you think he'll be willing to help? He's always been a bit of a recluse."

"I think so," I replied. "He's helped me before, and he knows the danger these creatures pose. Plus, he gave me the Metal Sigil. I think he wants us to succeed."

Daisy nodded. "That makes sense. And once we have his help, we can really start planning our attack on the goblins."

"Exactly," I said. "We'll use his knowledge of the forest to our advantage. Find the best routes, potential hiding spots, that sort of thing."

We continued eating and discussing our plans. The stew warmed us from the inside, and the company made the meal even more enjoyable. As we finished, I leaned back in my chair, feeling satisfied and content.

"This was delicious," I said. "Thanks for helping with dinner."

Daisy grinned. "Anytime. It's nice to have a good meal after all the excitement."

Caroline started gathering the empty bowls. "We should probably get some rest soon. Tomorrow's going to be a big day."

I stood up to help clear the table. "You're right. We need to be at our best when we talk to Harper and start planning our next move."

As we cleaned up the kitchen, the excitement for tomorrow's adventure hung in the air. The dishes clinked as we washed and dried them, our conversation drifting between recaps of the day's events and speculation about what we might face next.

With the kitchen clean and our bellies full, we made our way to the living room. The old couch creaked as we sat down, our bodies tired but our minds still active.

"So, what time should we head out tomorrow?" Daisy asked, stifling a yawn.

I thought for a moment. "Let's aim for early morning. I'm not sure if he would be able to set out right away — provided he's willing to help — but I'd rather have plenty of daylight left if that makes sense."

Caroline nodded. "Sounds good. I'll set an alarm."

As we sat there, the events of the day began to catch up with us. The adrenaline of our adventure had worn off, replaced by a deep tiredness. But underneath that fatigue was a current of excitement for what lay ahead.

"I gotta say, Sean," Daisy commented, "when you were lying on your stomach on that outcropping..." She licked her lips. "Shotgun in hand. That was... hmm... well, it was..."

"Hot," Caroline finished.

Daisy grinned and nodded. "Yeah... hot."

I laughed. "Well, hot as it might be, I'm feeling dirty and my muscles hurt."

Daisy and Caroline exchanged glances. "Well," Daisy said softly. "That right there might be two problems that we can solve for you..."

Chapter 11

As Daisy and Caroline giggled and pulled me to my feet, I felt both excited and intrigued. Their playful laughter filled the air as we made our way upstairs. It almost seemed like the two of them had plotted this out together and made this little plan when I hadn't been watching.

"Sean, you're gonna love this," Daisy said with

a wink, her blue eyes sparkling. "Ain't nothin' better than a hot shower after a long day outdoors."

"It's quite relaxing," Caroline agreed, her cheeks flushed.

As we entered the bathroom, they turned on the shower. Water cascaded in the background and steam began rising. I stood there with a grin on my lips, deciding to let them execute their little plan and surprise me.

"Alright," Daisy said. "Now stand still..." She exchanged a mischievous look with Caroline, and both girls came to me at the same time.

With teasing smiles, they began undressing me, their fingers working slowly and deliberately on each button and zipper. The softness of their touch sent shivers down my spine, while their whispered words of encouragement stoked the fire within me.

"Sean, looks like you have a few new muscles," Caroline murmured, her nerves disappearing and slowly making way for her kinkier side.

"It does," Daisy agreed. "All this hard work is doing you good, Sean." She grinned and shot me a wink.

I chuckled and spread my arms as the two of them undid my shirt. Then, Daisy got to her knees, unbuckled my belt, and pulled my pants and underwear down at the same time. Their teasing and feather-light touches had already made me hard, and both girls grinned as my cock sprang free.

"Into the shower with you," Daisy hummed. "We'll join you."

I stepped into the hot shower, the steam rising around me. As I adjusted to the warm water, I watched in fascination as they too began to undress. They removed their outdoors outfits. My pulse quickened as I took in the sight of their curves, their fair skin glistening under the bathroom lights while they stepped out of their panties and undid their bras.

Daisy was curvy but tall and fit, while Caroline was the textbook definition of 'thicc.' She had big, freckled breasts and a round, freckled butt. The two of them naked together was a sight straight from heaven, and my cock was fully erect in a moment as those two stepped into the shower with me.

"Come on, Sean," Daisy beckoned, her blonde hair falling in wet tendrils around her face. "Let's get you all cleaned up."

"Let us take care of you," Caroline added, her voice soft and sultry.

As they joined me in the shower, their naked bodies pressed against mine, I felt a surge of desire course through me. They began lathering me up, their soapy hands gliding over my skin. The sensation was electrifying, and as they giggled and whispered in my ears, I felt my tension melt away and make room for something else.

The warm water cascaded down my body, steam swirling around us as I reached out to take Daisy by the waist. She pressed against me eagerly, her blue eyes sparkling with mischief and desire. "My turn," I whispered, pulling her in for a deep, passionate kiss.

Caroline continued applying soap to my body, her hands lingering on my chest and shoulders as she watched Daisy and me intently. The combination of their touch sent shivers down my spine; it was almost too much to bear. But I wanted more.

"You gettin' nice and clean now?" Daisy teased between kisses.

"I think I'm just getting dirtier," I teased back.

As we continued to kiss, I let one hand roam over Daisy's wet, slick body until I found her firm, full breasts. I gently massaged them, savoring the feeling of her hardened nipples between my fingers. Daisy moaned into my mouth, urging me on.

Meanwhile, Caroline knelt before me, her green eyes locked onto mine as she took my cock into her mouth. Again, her brazenness when it came to this sort of thing took me by surprise, and I groaned with satisfaction at the sudden warmth and wetness. Her tongue danced along my shaft, teasing the sensitive underside before flicking across the tip. Every nerve ending felt alive, electric, as if I'd been plunged into a world of pure sensation.

"God, Caroline..." I breathed, unable to fully articulate the pleasure coursing through me.

As Caroline continued her ministrations, I kept

one hand on Daisy's breast, feeling her heartbeat quicken beneath my touch as I kneaded the deliciously soft breast. My other hand slipped between her thighs, gently brushing against her clit before tracing slow circles around it. Daisy's breath hitched, her body trembling ever so slightly as I continued to explore her most intimate area.

"Sean," she whispered, her voice laden with need. "That's… hmm… That's nice."

The steam from the hot water swirled around us, condensing on my skin and filling my lungs as I continued to pleasure Daisy. Her moans grew louder, her breaths coming in ragged gasps as she pressed herself against me. Meanwhile, Caroline sucked my cock with more vigor, bobbing her head as she took my full length into her eager mouth.

"Oh, Sean," Daisy panted, her voice full of lust, "you're makin' me feel so good."

"Good?" I whispered into her ear, my fingers moving faster within her slick folds. "I want you to feel incredible."

Daisy's body began to quiver, her grip on my shoulder tightening as she teetered on the edge of ecstasy. "Please, don't stop," she begged, her words punctuated by the soft, seductive sound of water cascading over our entwined forms.

"Sean," Caroline murmured, her lips still wrapped around my throbbing cock, "make her cum for you."

Her words, combined with the relentless pressure of her mouth on me, pushed me further toward the brink. Desperate to hold on, I focused all my attention on Daisy, feeling her body tense and tighten around my probing fingers.

And then, with a cry that echoed off the tiled walls of the shower, she shattered, her orgasm washing over her. "Y-yes!" she cried out, her body shaking with the force of her climax. "Oh, Sean... Oh, fuck!"

I grinned and doubled down, making her squirm and moan. But having the pretty blonde cum under my touch only made me that much more turned on, and the sensation of Caroline's mouth on me became impossible to ignore any longer.

"Caroline," I gasped, my voice strained with urgency, "I'm gonna cum."

She looked up at me with those green eyes, full of mischief. She pulled me out of her mouth and guided my cock between her large, freckled breasts, jiggling them around me as I reached the point of no return.

"Give it to her, Sean," Daisy panted. "Make a mess of her."

The sight of Caroline's chest, slick with water and soap, combined with Daisy's encouragement, was too much for me to bear. With a guttural groan, I let go, my cum splattering across Caroline's ample, freckled bosom. Halfway through, she aimed it at Daisy's smooth stomach, who gave a satisfied meep as a rope of seed landed on her.

"Look at that mess," Daisy purred, her eyes alight with satisfaction. "You really know how to treat your girls, don't you, Sean? Good thing we're under the shower!"

As the last waves of pleasure coursed through me, I chuckled and gave her a wet smack on her butt.

But I wasn't done yet.

Caroline's eyes met mine, and she saw it. She

gave an excited giggle, her chest heaving with anticipation.

"Your turn," I murmured, my voice low and commanding. With one strong arm, I lifted Caroline to her feet and gently pushed her against the tiled wall of the shower.

She offered no resistance, only a look of pure desire as I knelt behind her. My hands gripped her wide hips, and I was greeted with the beautiful sight of her freckled butt. Soap and water clung to her body, making her shiny and even more inviting.

"Sean..." she breathed shakily, her entire body quivering with anticipation. As my tongue flicked over her wet folds, she gasped, her fingers grabbing the wall for support. I could feel her growing need, her body desperate for release. She was wet and close.

"Please... don't stop."

I glanced over at Daisy, who stood watching us with rapt attention. Her blue eyes were dark with lust as she hummed her admiration. "So beautiful," she said softly.

Caroline's moans grew louder, echoing off the

walls as I continued to lick and tease her sensitive flesh. Within moments, her legs began to tremble, and with a cry, her body shuddered as she found her release.

"Oh, Sean!" she cried out. "Yes! Oh! I'm cumming, Sean!"

Daisy grinned, stepping closer. "That… hmm…" she just purred.

"Ready for more?" I asked, my voice a growl as I stood and motioned for Daisy to join Caroline against the wall. She complied with an excited giggle, pressing her body beside Caroline's.

"Come here, baby," Daisy whispered, her blue eyes meeting mine as I positioned myself behind her, my hard cock pressed against her lower back. With her harem sister still recovering from her orgasm next to her, I kissed her neck, and she leaned into my embrace.

Then, with one hand on her hip and the other braced against the wall, I entered her tight and wet pussy, our bodies moving in sync as the water continued to pour down upon us.

"Ah, Sean!" Daisy moaned, her head falling back onto my shoulder as I buried myself within her welcoming warmth.

My heart raced as I thrust deep. The sound of our bodies connecting filled the steamy air, and her moans only served to fuel my arousal. Seeing Caroline's eager gaze watching us, I couldn't resist the temptation to switch my attention to her.

"Caroline," I panted, pulling out of Daisy and stepping towards her, "your turn."

"Yes, please!" she stammered, her green eyes wide with anticipation.

I lined myself up with her entrance, and in one smooth motion, slid inside her. Her voluptuous form jiggled with each thrust, and her ample butt cheeks bounced enticingly before me. I was captivated by the sight, and the feel of her wetness enveloping me only heightened my desire.

"Sean, oh God, y-yes," Caroline moaned, clearly reveling in the pleasure. "More! Pull my hair, please!"

Damn. I loved her.

With a grin, I reached up, grabbing a handful of her damp red hair and tugged gently at first, gauging her reaction. When she cried out for more, I pulled harder, sending a shiver down her spine.

"Fuck, this is so good, Caroline," I grunted as I continued to pound into her, her body pressed against the shower wall. I could feel the pressure building within me, my orgasm approaching rapidly.

Daisy, still beside us, watched intently, her lips curling into a sultry smile. "Cum in her, baby," she purred. "Give her what she needs."

"Yes!" Caroline called out. "Cum for me, Sean! Oh… I want it!"

Unable to hold back any longer, I released a guttural moan as my climax washed over me. I felt my cock pulse and throb as I emptied myself inside Caroline, my vision momentarily blurred by the intensity of the pleasure. The sensation of her warm, wet walls clenching around me as I came was unlike anything I had ever experienced.

She was trembling under the force of it, and Daisy ran a soft hand over my arm, licking her lips in delight at the sound.

My breathing labored, I slowly pulled out of Caroline, my knees weak from the powerful orgasm. I leaned forward, bracing myself against the tiled wall, and drew in a deep breath as the steam surrounded me.

"That was crazy hot," Daisy hummed.

"You two were right," I sighed, turning to face Daisy and Caroline who stood beside me under the shower spray. "This was *exactly* what I needed."

Caroline laughed, and Daisy grinned, her wet blonde hair clinging to her cheeks. "Told you it'd do the trick, didn't I?" Her blue eyes sparkled with mischief and delight.

"Right now, all I want to do is lie in bed and be lazy," I admitted, feeling the warmth of their bodies close to mine. It was comforting, almost like a blanket made of pure affection. "Maybe go for another round after a while."

"Sounds perfect," Daisy agreed, reaching out to trace her fingers along my back. "We could all use some rest after that."

"Uh-huh," Caroline nodded, her green eyes locked on mine. "I'm up for some cuddling."

I grinned. "Cuddling sounds perfect."

A few moments later, we stepped out of the shower together, our fingers intertwined, and headed toward the bedroom to laze about and — after half an hour — go for another round...

Chapter 12

The next morning, I woke well-rested. The bed was empty, meaning the girls were already downstairs. Last night's romp had left me feeling revitalized, and I was looking forward to continuing the plans we had made.

Sunlight peeked through the curtains as I got dressed. I could hear Daisy moving around downstairs, and the shower was running, so I took it Caroline was in there. The events of yesterday still fresh in my mind, I headed to the kitchen.

Daisy stood at the counter, pouring coffee into mugs. The morning light made her golden hair look radiant, and I admired the view until she caught me looking and shot me a smile over her shoulder.

"Morning, mister," she said. "Want some?"

"Always," I replied, taking a mug as I pinched her firm butt cheek, making her giggle. "I'm thinking of heading out to talk to Harper about the goblins right away. I want to get things moving."

Caroline walked in, her hair damp. "That's a good idea," she said. "Mind if I stay here and keep an eye on things? Your house is better for quiet research than mine."

I grinned. "You're always welcome here, Caroline. And you, too, Daisy."

The girls shot me warm looks, and I kissed them each on the cheek before I had a quick breakfast and got dressed. A few minutes later, I grabbed my keys and headed out to my red Ford pickup.

The morning air was cool and crisp, and I took a deep breath.

I stepped into the car, started the engine, and drove towards Harper's place on the outskirts of town. It was a nice drive down the countryside, and I listened to a few local stations, where people talked about little nothings that were entertaining or informative. Nothing much happened out here, and the world sometimes seemed far away.

Just the way I liked it.

After I drove through Waycross, Harper's small house came into view, surrounded by trees. I parked and walked up to the weathered front door, knocking firmly.

After a moment, Harper opened the door. His long gray hair was tied back into a ponytail, and his beard was as bushy as ever. "Sean," he said. "What brings you by so early?"

"Morning, Harper," I said. "Need to talk about the goblins near my property. It's getting worse."

Harper peeked down the lane, then nodded and stepped aside. "Come in, have a seat. I was expecting things might get worse before they got better."

I entered the cottage. Old furniture and trinkets filled the space, and I sat in a worn armchair that creaked under my weight. Harper went into the kitchen to get us both a mug of strong tea — not a coffee man, apparently — and he handed me mine before he sat down in a comfy chair opposite me.

"So," he began, "what is it you wanted to discuss?"

I had considered on the ride in whether I wanted Harper in the circle of people who knew about my magic. Since we were asking for help, and the situation might call for my magic, I reckoned it was wisest to tell him now and not surprise him with it later.

"Well, first off," I began, "there's something I want to share with you. Those Sigils that I have — the wood one and the metal one you gave me — they have unlocked some kind of ability in me."

He perked an eyebrow. "An *ability*, huh?"

"Yeah," I said. "Magic. It allows me to manipulate the corresponding materials — wood and metals. We also found a Portal Sigil that allows me to open gateways to... well, to other realms."

To my own ears, it still sounded something like madness, but Harper just cracked a broad grin and slowly nodded. "I knew it," he hummed. "I knew… I just *knew* it couldn't all be nonsense!"

Now it was my turn to raise an eyebrow. "What do you mean?" I asked.

"The magic!" he said, throwing out his hands. "There are legends of it here in Waycross. And I always knew those legends couldn't be total nonsense. And now here you are, a practitioner of those arts!" He chuckled and shook his head. "I always knew it was all true."

For a moment, I was a little surprised. But it was pleasant that he was on board — that I didn't have to prove anything. Interesting, too, that this person whom — in my previous life and occupation — I would've thought this man to be a little crazy. It just shows that sometimes, a little less judgment is to the benefit of all. He didn't seem to be judgmental himself, and he didn't even ask me to prove it — just took my word for it.

I smiled. "Well, I'm happy you're so accepting of it," I said. "This conversation could've gone differently…"

"Oh no," he said and chuckled. "I feel like I've been waiting all my life for this." He shot me a genuinely warm look. "It fascinates me. Anything I can do to help, Sean. I always thought I'd seen it all, and what you just told me opens up a whole new world for me."

I nodded, thinking for a moment. "Well, in that case," I said, "the girls and I used the Portal Sigil to travel to a place called Harrwick. We met a witch there, and we helped her by defeating a troll."

Harper leaned forward. "You killed a troll, you say? Tell me more."

I recounted our adventure, from finding the troll's lair to setting traps and defeating it. After that, I told him how Greida had bolstered my magic, making it innate instead of based on the grimoire. Harper listened intently, nodding occasionally.

When I finished, Harper stroked his beard. "You've been busy. Done well, too. In fact, it sounds like you have it all under control."

"Well, not all of it. We need a good tracker, Harper. Someone who knows the forest. I want to go after those goblins. I need Waycross to be safe for its people, and I need my home to be safe for me and my women and my son."

Harper nodded. "I can help. I want to. Know the forest well. We'll need a strategy, though. It's rained last night, and unless you have a set of tracks right now, there's nothing for us to follow." Harper rubbed his chin. "Might not be what you wanna hear, but the best way is to wait for them to appear. Then we can follow them back. Might take some time, though."

I nodded. "I'll watch for any activity. As soon as they show up, I'll come get you. We'll need to move fast once we have a lead."

"Good plan," Harper said, standing up. "I'll get some supplies ready in the meantime. Make sure I'm ready to set out the moment you come knocking."

I gave a firm nod, pleased with his eagerness to help. We spoke a while longer, and Harper told me a little bit more about his experience tracking. It turned out he used to take hunting parties into the woods nearer Blackhill and was an expert guide and hunter. Before that, he was Army like most of his ancestors had been. It was good – just the kind of skills we would need out there.

Finally, the tea was gone, and I didn't want to bother Harper any longer than was necessary. He wasn't a people person, that much was clear, so I wanted to give him time for himself to prepare. I stood, and he rose as well.

"Thanks for your help, Harper," I said. "We'll be in touch as soon as we spot any goblins."

Harper extended his hand, and I shook it. "Take care, Sean. We'll sort out those goblins soon enough."

With that, I headed back to my truck, leaving Harper's rustic abode with plenty to think about on the drive home.

Chapter 13

I parked my truck in the driveway and stepped out, blinking at the bright morning sun.

The cool breeze carried the scent of pine and damp earth, and I took a deep breath, letting the familiar smells of home wash over me. The meeting with Harper had gone well, and I felt good about our plan to deal with the goblins.

As I walked up to the house, I could see Daisy and Caroline through the window. They were in the kitchen, busy organizing our supplies from the latest adventure. I opened the front door and stepped inside.

"Hey, I'm back," I called out as I strolled through the living room and into the kitchen where the girls were.

Daisy looked up from a pile of gear on the kitchen table. "How'd it go with Harper?"

"Pretty good," I replied. "He's on board to help us track the goblins."

Caroline smiled broadly. "That's great news. Did you make a plan?"

I was about to answer when my phone buzzed in my pocket. I pulled it out and saw Brooke's name on the screen. My stomach did a little flip.

"Hold on, it's Brooke," I said to the girls. I answered the call as I walked into the living room, leaving the girls in the kitchen as they exchanged knowing looks and giggled.

"Hey, Brooke," I said.

"Hi, Sean," Brooke said. "Is this a bad time?"

I walked up to one of the windows and peeked

out, surveying my property as we spoke. "Not at all," I said. "What's up?"

"Well, Cody's been asking about visiting you," Brooke said. "I was wondering if we could come over tomorrow?"

Her voice carried that same wistful sound that it had carried before. I could tell that our last conversation bothered her — I knew her well enough for that. That was a good thing, though. It meant that she was working it out, coming to a decision of what she wanted. I had faith in our love and the strength of our bond, and I knew she would make the right choice this time.

A smile spread across my face, and I tried to sound as casual as I could — I did not want to put pressure on her. "I'd love that. I'll get everything in order here."

"He misses you," Brooke said. "He's been talking about you non-stop."

"I miss him too," I replied. "I've been working on making the house safe and welcoming for when you both visit."

There was a pause on the other end of the line. "I'm glad to hear that," Brooke said. "I've been thinking a lot about what you told me. About your... abilities."

I took a deep breath. "How are you feeling about all that?"

"I'm still trying to process it," Brooke admitted. "It's a lot to take in, but I'm doing my best to understand."

"I appreciate that," I said. "I know it's not easy."

"I meant what I said in my letter," Brooke continued. "I want to try and make things work between us again. There's this feeling deep inside me that tells me that this is what's right."

Her words made my heart beat a little faster. "It is. And I want that too," I said. "But Brooke, you need to know that you have time for this decision, okay? You can come to terms — or not — with everything at your own speed. Don't rush things, okay? We'll do it right."

I could hear her swallow, and I imagined her smiling softly on the other end of the line. "You're right. Let's take it slow," Brooke suggested. "But I want to try and stay at your house — at least for a night."

I blinked, taking a moment to process that. It

was great news, honestly — a step in the right direction. "Yeah," I said. "Sure, Brooke. I mean, I'd love to have you over!"

"Great!" she said, her voice a little stronger and more enthusiastic now. "I feel that — you know, if I spend some time there — things may become more familiar. I mean, right now, I'm making a decision based on nothing. I just want to be closer — to see if it can be a safe place for us." She sighed, then released a small chuckle as if some burden slipped from her shoulders. "So, let's try. Just one night. See how it feels."

"That sounds great to me," I agreed. "I'll make sure everything's ready for you both. I have a guest room for you, and you and Cody can share it. He normally sleeps in my room, but I'm thinking you'd prefer him with you, right?"

"You know me well," she said, smile in her voice. "Yes. For now, I'd like that."

"Great! We have a deal."

"Thank you, Sean," Brooke said. "We'll see you tomorrow then."

"Looking forward to it," I replied.

We said our goodbyes and ended the call. I

stood in the living room for a moment, processing the conversation. The thought of seeing Cody again filled me with excitement. And the possibility of reconnecting with Brooke gave me hope. If she was going to spend the night here, it was more progress than I'd dared hope for.

I walked back into the kitchen. Daisy and Caroline looked up at me expectantly. They both had smiles on their faces that made me chuckle.

"How was Brooke?" Daisy asked, perking a dark blonde eyebrow.

I laughed. "She was good. She and Cody are coming over tomorrow. They're both staying the night. I'd like for you both to be here too, if that's okay with you. I really think you need to meet Brooke."

Caroline turned a little red at the prospect of people coming over. "Oh, of course! Uh, yeah, that's great news!" she said, her nervousness returning a little. "I, uh… Yeah, that's really nice!"

I could see she meant it, but as someone with a shy nature, the idea of having Brooke here was perhaps a little daunting. Luckily, she had some time to mentally prepare. I was happy she wasn't bowing out by saying she'd rather not be here.

"I'd love to get to know her better," Daisy hummed, already pondering the encounter. "She seems nice!"

"And, uh, it'll help her make her decision, right?" Caroline added.

"Exactly," I said. I looked around the room, suddenly aware of all the work we still needed to do. "We should make sure everything's perfect for their visit."

Daisy stood up. "Don't worry, we'll help you get the place ready."

Caroline nodded in agreement. "Yeah... Just, uh, tell us what needs to be done."

I felt a wave of gratitude for their support. "Thanks, girls. Let's start by finishing up with these supplies, then we can focus on cleaning the place and getting the guest room ready."

"Where do we start?" Daisy asked, already standing up. "There's so much to do."

I scratched my chin, considering our options. "We should tidy up and get the guest room ready for Cody and Brooke. Make it welcoming, you know?"

Caroline stood up, brushing off her jeans. "I'll take care of the guest room. Make sure everything's in order."

"I'll help you with that," Daisy chimed in. "We'll make it nice and cozy for them."

I nodded, feeling a weight lift off my shoulders. "Great. While you two handle that, I'll use my magic to run by the doors and make sure everything is nice and sturdy and in a good state of repair. Just for extra security. This place needs to be the safest it can be."

The girls headed upstairs, their footsteps fading as they discussed how to arrange the guest room. I turned my attention to the front door, focusing on my Sigil Magic.

Energy coursed through my body as I concentrated on the wood and metal elements of the door and the windows. Of course, it had only been a short while since I'd done my initial run of making the house as goblin-proof as it could be, but I used my Sigil Magic on every element to make sure that it was the best it could be.

As I worked, my mind constantly drifted to tomorrow's visit. I was excited to see Cody, but I also felt nervous about seeing Brooke again. I really hoped that this visit would be a step toward rebuilding our relationship. I had a feeling it would, but I wasn't the type to leave anything to chance, so I wanted the place to be perfect. Every lock and window and door and alarm was going to be as sturdy as Sigil Magic could make it.

After finishing with the first floor, I made my way upstairs to join Daisy and Caroline in the guest room. They had already made significant progress, arranging the beds and placing fresh linens on them.

"Wow, this looks fantastic," I said, stepping into the room. "Thanks for all your help with this."

Daisy grinned, fluffing a pillow. "It's no trouble at all, baby. We want everythin' to be just right for Cody and Brooke. We know this is important for you."

I shot her an appreciative look as Caroline turned to me, her head tilted slightly. "Are you nervous about seeing Brooke again?"

I paused, considering her question. "I wouldn't say nervous," I finally concluded. "I've known her far too long and far too well to be nervous when she's near. In fact, she has the opposite effect, like a good wife should." I shook my head. "No, not nervous. I think 'hopeful' is a better word. I think this visit could be a good step forward for us. I don't want things to go poorly, so I'm leaving nothing to chance. But I also know I can't directly force someone to feel a certain way, you know? If she concludes that this life isn't safe enough for her, then that's her decision." I shrugged. "But honestly, knowing Brooke, I think that's not what will happen."

Daisy and Caroline exchanged a look. "Well, we'll make sure to give y'all some space," Daisy said. "I reckon you should have some time alone with Brooke. Make sure you get to talk about the things you two need to talk about and all."

"I appreciate that," I replied. "But I also want you both to meet her properly. Get to know each other a bit."

Caroline nodded, adjusting the curtains. "Of course. W-we're looking forward to meeting her."

It was sweet. She was trying really hard to be casual about the whole thing. But if *anyone* was nervous, it was sweet, sweet Caroline. It still amazed me how she could be such a wild one in private and such a shy girl when others were around. Hopefully, she'd feel comfortable around Brooke soon enough.

"Oh, we'll be around for that, baby," Daisy added, "but we can head out for a while if you need privacy."

"That sounds perfect," I said, feeling grateful for their understanding. "I want this to be a comfortable visit for everyone involved."

We continued discussing the details of the visit, making sure we had everything covered. The girls were eager to help make the day special for Cody and Brooke.

As the afternoon wore on, I felt more prepared for tomorrow. The guest room looked inviting, and the added security measures gave me peace of mind. With Daisy and Caroline's support, I was confident that Cody and Brooke's visit would be a positive experience for all of us.

We went to bed early that night after we'd fixed up the house, picked up groceries at Earl's, and made sure everything was in order. This was the third night in a row that both girls spent at my place, and we were starting to feel more and more like a unit — like a family. I loved every second of it, and I could tell the girls did, too.

It was my secret hope that they'd both move in with me, eventually. We could keep Daisy's farm, of course, but I wouldn't mind if Caroline brought her stuff over and terminated her lease. As I held them close that night after making love, I knew I never wanted to let go of them again.

Chapter 14 (Caroline)

Caroline stirred, the weight of sleep fading as her mind gradually woke.

It was still deep in the night — dark out. She felt his warm body against her — Sean — with Daisy sleeping soundly on his other side. They had had a wild night, exploring fantasies of a kind that made Caroline blush and bite her lip as she thought back to them.

With that, she was wide awake.

The soft sound of Sean's steady breathing filled the room, and the warmth of his body against hers was comforting, but her thoughts were too restless to let her sink back into sleep. She lay still for a moment, staring into the darkness, listening to the quiet of the house. Everything felt so calm, but inside, her mind was whirling.

Tomorrow. Brooke would be here tomorrow.

The thought sent a ripple of anxiety through her, a tightness settling in her chest. Brooke wasn't just anyone. She was Sean's past — his ex-wife, the mother of his child. And now, she was coming here, to this house, to meet the women who had stepped into Sean's life after their separation. The weight of it pressed down on her, making her stomach churn.

Daisy seemed so easy-going about it. Caroline had always thought the bubbly blonde was such a strong and radiant woman — unaffected by anything. Before Sean, they had spoken on occasion, but Daisy wasn't a library-going girl, and Caroline didn't spend much time at the social venues of Waycross and Blackhill, so they had never been more than acquaintances.

And now, they were slowly becoming friends... More like sisters. Who share the same man. Who could've thought that Daisy would've been so open to it? There had always been talk about her father and his 'three wives,' but Caroline had just thought it was a rumor. And if it wasn't, what concern was it of hers?

But now, Daisy had proven to be not only an unshakably positive person but also someone who didn't care in the least about gossip or appearances — as long as she and the people she loved were happy... Caroline really admired her.

Caroline's eyes drifted toward the window, where the faint silver light of the moon spilled through the curtains. With careful movement, she slipped out from under the covers, mindful not to wake Sean or Daisy.

The bed creaked slightly as she rose, and she froze, waiting to see if either of them stirred. When they didn't, she padded softly across the room, the wooden floor cool beneath her feet as she reached for her robe and pulled it around her shoulders.

The house was so quiet. She glanced back at the bed, at the peaceful rise and fall of Sean's chest, the way Daisy's blonde hair fanned out against the pillow. They were both so calm, so at ease. Caroline wished she could feel the same.

Her thoughts still churning, she made her way downstairs, each step careful and deliberate to keep the stairs from creaking too loudly. The familiar surroundings of the house comforted her; Sean's place was already beginning to feel like home. She crossed the living room and entered the kitchen, the soft shine of moonlight through the windows giving the space a faint, silvery light.

Caroline reached for a glass from the cabinet and filled it with water from the tap. She brought the glass to her lips, taking slow sips as she leaned against the counter, her thoughts returning to Brooke.

Brooke.

The name hung in her mind, and Caroline found herself feeling something she hadn't expected. It wasn't just anxiety. It was curiosity. What would she be like? Sean had talked about her, of course, shared memories of their time together, but meeting her in person – getting to know her – was different. Brooke wasn't just some abstract figure from Sean's past – she was a living, breathing part of his life, and she was coming here tomorrow.

Caroline knew she couldn't help but feel a little nervous about it. Would Brooke see her as an intruder? Would she judge her for being part of Sean's life now, for being in a relationship with him and Daisy? The thought made her chest tighten with apprehension. She didn't want to come across as someone who was trying to replace Brooke or take her place in Sean's heart. That wasn't her role.

But what *was* her role?

She sighed softly, setting the glass down on the counter and looking out the window. The woods stretched beyond the yard, dark and still under the moonlight.

She'd spent so much of her life feeling like she was on the sidelines, content to observe, to keep herself in the background. But things had changed when she met Sean. She'd found a part of herself she didn't even know existed — a part that wanted to be seen, to be valued, to have a place in this strange, wonderful relationship they had formed.

And Sean had given her that. He had made her feel important, cherished, in a way she hadn't expected. He'd welcomed her into his life, made her part of something bigger than herself. He was so open, so patient, so honest. Everything about him radiated calm strength, and it drew Caroline in like a magnet. She *loved* him. Deeply. She could be who she was with him.

And now, Brooke was coming.

Caroline knew Brooke would always have a special place in Sean's heart. They shared a history, a child. That bond would never go away. But that didn't mean there wasn't room for her. It didn't mean she didn't have a place here too.

She took another sip of water, letting the cool liquid soothe her throat as her thoughts settled. Yes, Brooke was important to Sean. But so was she. So was Daisy. And Sean had made it clear that he wanted all of them in his life. This wasn't about competition — it was about love, about building something new together. Brooke had her place, just as Caroline did.

She thought about Sean, about the way he held her, the way he looked at her with that quiet intensity that made her feel like she was the only person in the world.

He loved her. She knew that, deep down, even if she sometimes doubted herself.

And Daisy — Daisy had this effortless grace that Caroline admired, this warmth that made everything feel lighter, easier, *funnier*. Together, they were building something real, something strong. She couldn't let herself feel threatened by Brooke's arrival.

Instead, she needed to be *open* to it. She needed to treat the situation like Sean would, with quiet and calm confidence. To go into a situation prepared and ready, open to let things play out. No pressure, no stress, no anxiety. Just see if it works — trust that it will.

Caroline took a deep breath, the weight in her chest beginning to lift. She couldn't control how Brooke would feel or what she would think of their relationship, but she could control how *she* approached it. She would be herself — kind, open, and willing to make this work.

She finished her glass of water and set it down in the sink, her decision made. Tomorrow, she would meet Brooke with an open heart, and whatever happened, she wouldn't change who she was. Sean had made her feel valued, and she wasn't going to let her insecurities get in the way of that.

Not this time. Her life would no longer be dictated by fears.

Caroline took one last look out at the dark woods, feeling a sense of calm settle over her. She turned and headed back up the stairs, her steps lighter now. When she reached the bedroom, she slipped back into bed, careful not to disturb Sean or Daisy. The warmth of the covers enveloped her, and she felt Sean's arm instinctively wrap around her waist as he shifted closer, pulling her into the familiar comfort of his embrace.

As she settled back into the bed, Caroline smiled softly to herself. Whatever tomorrow brought, she knew one thing for sure — she was exactly where she was meant to be.

Chapter 15

I stood on the porch, watching the driveway.

I wasn't nervous, but I *was* a little excited. This was going to be an important moment for all of us — something that would influence the days to come. But we — the girls and I — had done everything we could to make this go as smoothly as possible.

The early afternoon air was balmy, and the sky was a bright blue. The coming few days were looking to be beautiful, maybe with a little rain now and then to keep things fresh and green.

It was looking to be a good time for us all.

I heard the familiar rumble of Brooke's black sedan before I saw it. My heart beat faster as the vehicle came into view, kicking up dust behind it. Her city car wasn't really made for roads like these, but Brooke was an excellent driver. Despite her trying the corporate and city angle, she was still a red-blooded, small-town American just like I was, and she knew how to handle a vehicle. She could drive a Tesla through the swamp and still come out with nothing but a little muck on the tires.

Well, maybe I was exaggerating. But just a little.

I smiled as she pulled to a stop in the clearing in front of my house. She killed the engine, and then the doors swung open.

I saw Brooke first, because she was on my side of the car. Her black hair shone in the sunlight, and she looked even more beautiful than she had last time. She wore tight, high-waisted jeans with boots and a light blouse with the top buttons undone, displaying the cleavage that, despite having explored it a thousand times with my lips, I could never get enough of.

Her blue eyes met mine, and I felt a rush of emotions. A moment later, Cody jumped out of the car, full of energy. He blazed his way to me, his eyes bright with excitement, and he just kept shouting "Dad, dad, dad!"

Laughing, I crouched as he raced up the steps to the porch and enclosed him in a tight hug. "Hey, buddy," I said, holding him close and pressing a kiss to his forehead, his familiar scent soothing me. "I really missed you!"

"I missed you too, Dad!" he said. "Can I go to Daisy's and get Tink?" he asked.

I laughed. Leave it to a kid to be able to pick up where he left off, even if it was days ago. "Daisy's already here, buddy. I think Tink is in the fields. Why don't you go look for her?"

"Okay!" He loosened himself from the embrace and darted off, leaving me to rise and look at Brooke's shapely figure as she came up the stairs to the porch with a radiant smile.

"Hey, you," I said softly, reaching out to embrace her.

"Hey," she replied as she met my embrace and gave me a soft kiss on the cheek. "I missed you, Sean," she said.

"I missed you too, Brooke," I replied. It felt good to have her here, especially now that she was staying. "Come on in," I said. I pointed towards the house. "I've made a few improvements since you last saw it."

"We don't need to wait for Cody?"

"Oh, he knows his way around," I said. "Tink is frolicking somewhere; Cody knows her haunts. He loves that dog."

She smiled and nodded, then followed me inside. She looked around at the wooden paneling and the furniture in the living room. Having a visitor always made me look at my own place as if through a stranger's eyes, and I had to admit the place was looking cozy — like a real home.

"It looks great, Sean," Brooke said. "You've done a lot with the place."

"Thanks," I replied. I led her through the hallway. "I wanted to make it feel like home, you know?"

Brooke stopped and looked at the reinforced windows and strong locks. She raised an eyebrow. "These are new," she said.

"Yeah," I said. I nodded. "Just some added security measures. You can never be too careful out here."

She nodded. "Well, I'm happy to see it," she said. "Safety is important, and it's really good that you're taking it all seriously."

"You know I do, Brooke," I said. "You and Cody are important to me. More important to me than myself. I need you to be safe, and I will do what I need to achieve that."

She reached over and squeezed my arm for a moment before she looked around the room. Her eyes lingered on the couch and coffee table. "I like it," she said quietly. "It's cozy."

"Well, come sit with me, then," I said. "It's your home for the day. And for tomorrow. For as long as you want to stay."

She smiled, and we sat down on the couch. The leather creaked beneath us as we settled in. She was still looking around, taking in the place. But I could see she liked it.

She chuckled softly. "It's very *you*," she said. "Looks like the place you always dreamed about."

"*We* always dreamed about," I corrected her. "You were there, remember?"

She laughed, a sound that brought back such great memories — memories I hoped we would be making more of. "Yeah," she said. "That's true." She gave me a warm and easy look. "Those were the days, huh?"

"We will see them again, Brooke. We will."

There was a brief, comfortable silence between us, and then I rose. "How about some coffee?" I asked. "I made a fresh pot."

"That sounds great, Sean," she hummed.

"Alright," I said, rising to head into the kitchen. "I'll be right back."

I poured two mugs of coffee, my mind still churning with the excitement I felt at Brooke's return. As I carried them back into the living room, Brooke was sitting with her legs tucked beneath her, eyes wandering over the room like she was taking everything in.

When she noticed me, she gave a small smile, but there was something thoughtful behind it. I had a feeling we were about to explore what she was thinking.

"Here you go," I said, handing her a mug.

"Thanks." She took it with both hands, inhaling deeply before taking a sip. I sat back down next to her, keeping a bit of space between us but close enough that our knees almost touched.

"So, what do you think of the place now that you've had a good look?" I asked, sipping my own coffee.

She let out a soft laugh. "Honestly? It's more than I expected. I mean, not that I mean *you* couldn't do it, but more like… well, I suppose in my mind I made small-town life a little less than it actually is."

I grinned and nodded. "And big-city life a little *more* than it actually is."

"Yeah," she agreed. "You've really made this place into a home, Sean. The improvements… the security. It's solid, and I feel it. It's good to see you're taking it so seriously."

"I have to," I said, meeting her eyes. "Especially

now. Cody, you… I want you both to feel safe here, just like I do. I've put a lot of thought into how to make sure nothing can get in — whether it's natural or magical."

She gave a slight nod, a flicker of relief crossing her face. "That means a lot. Cody and I… we had a long talk the other night, actually." Her voice softened as she shifted slightly, placing her coffee mug on the low coffee table in front of the couch.

I tilted my head, curiosity piqued. "Yeah? What about?"

She paused for a moment, eyes glancing toward the window as if weighing her words. "He told me he doesn't really like living in Louisville." Her fingers traced the rim of the mug. "Said he misses the space, the freedom here. I guess the city isn't really… home for him. I've been wondering how much of that was because of me."

I set my mug down on the table, leaning forward slightly. "I had a feeling he might feel that way. He's always been happier out here. The open space, Tink, being able to run around… This place gives him a lot of what Louisville can't." Then, I reached out and touched her knee, making her look at me. "But that's not because of *you*, Brooke. Don't blame yourself. It's just who he is. He's a kid who loves nature, the country, animals." I shook my head. "Not a city boy."

Brooke sighed, her shoulders relaxing a bit as if saying it out loud helped. "Yeah, I think so too. He said he feels more at ease here. It's just... I don't know, Sean. It's hard. I've been trying to do what's best for him — give him structure, security. But it's becoming more and more obvious that what he really needs is space to be himself."

She looked at me, and for the first time, there was that familiar vulnerability in her eyes, the one I used to see when she was unsure if she was doing the right thing.

I squeezed her knee. "You're doing your best, Brooke. You always have. And it's not easy being in the city — especially with everything going on in our lives. I get why you thought it was the right move, but I'm really glad you talked to him about it. It's better to know now than to let it keep bothering him."

She smiled softly, her eyes warming a bit. "Thanks for saying that. It helps hearing it from you. He's all I think about most days… and I think I've been too wrapped up in trying to protect him from the unknowns. But hearing him say he's unhappy there… it's hard to ignore that."

She paused for a moment, then added quietly, "I'd love for him to spend more time here. Maybe even... well, when things settle down with this magical threat, maybe it's something I should seriously consider for both of us."

I couldn't stop the smile that broke across my face. "I think that's a great idea, Brooke. I want you both to spend more time here. And not just because of the danger out there, but because this place feels like where you and Cody belong."

Her fingers brushed mine as she lowered her coffee mug to the table. "I'd love that too, Sean. When things calm down... I want to spend more time here. Maybe figure out how we can make this work. For Cody, for us."

I nodded, heart thudding a little faster at the possibility of her and Cody being part of this life again. "I think we can do that, Brooke."

My heart was pumping fast. Still, there were things we needed to discuss before we could move on. My relationship with Caroline and Daisy was a big thing, and I was not going to give up either of those girls. Brooke would need to know that.

Chapter 16

After a full afternoon of playing with Cody and hanging around the house, the five of us gathered around the dining table in my kitchen. Daisy and Caroline had arranged for candles, and their gentle glow softened the hard lines and created a cozy atmosphere.

The rich scent of roasted chicken, buttery

mashed potatoes, and fresh vegetables filled the room, mingling with the faintest hint of spice from the gravy Daisy had made — an old family recipe. Cody sat beside me, practically bouncing in his seat as he eyed the food, his excitement obvious in the way he gripped his fork in anticipation.

Daisy had outdone herself, and I knew she was proud of the meal. She and Caroline had spent most of the afternoon cooking while I had spent time in the field with Brooke, Cody, and Tink. Now, as we sat down together, the table laden with food, I knew the girls had given it their everything.

Cody's eyes widened as he reached for the platter of chicken. "Can I have the drumstick, Dad?"

I chuckled, nodding as I passed the plate his way. "Go ahead, buddy. Just make sure to save some for the rest of us."

He grinned and eagerly took the biggest drumstick, nearly dropping it onto his plate in his haste.

Brooke, sitting across from us, smiled softly, watching him with a mother's fondness. Her blue eyes flicked over to me, and for a brief moment, we shared a look — one of those small, quiet moments of connection, like we'd had so many times before.

"Everything looks wonderful," Brooke said, turning to Daisy and Caroline. "You two really went all out. I've eaten at more fancy restaurants than I care to count, but I don't think I've had anything that smells as good as this."

Daisy beamed, already dishing out mashed potatoes onto everyone's plates. "Oh, don't be silly! This is just a little something I whipped up. Honestly, cooking for a crowd is more fun than cooking for myself."

Caroline, seated at the other end of the table, gave a small, proud smile as she helped spoon out the roasted vegetables. "Daisy's kind of the master chef around here. I'm just her assistant."

I smiled at that. She seemed to have conquered her shyness for tonight, and I really appreciated the effort she put in. She was a great woman, and I loved her all the more for it.

Brooke raised an eyebrow, glancing between the two of them. "Well, I'm impressed. I can barely handle spaghetti without something going wrong."

"You should've seen me last week," I added, grinning as I grabbed the gravy boat and poured a generous amount over my potatoes. "I tried to grill some steaks, but I got distracted. Let's just say we were lucky Daisy had leftovers in the fridge."

Daisy laughed, shaking her head. "Burnt to a crisp! I swear, Sean, you're great with a gun and all, but you really need to work on your timing when it comes to food." She waved a spoon at me. "Just don't get distracted and start doin' other stuff and you'll be fine. You're a natural at cookin'."

Cody giggled beside me, biting into his drumstick with a loud crunch. "Dad, remember the casserole?"

Brooke chuckled, giving me a playful look as she added some vegetables to her plate. "I had to throw away that dish…"

I laughed. "Well, at least I didn't burn down the house," I quipped, which earned a round of laughter from everyone.

As the conversation continued, we settled into

the meal, the clinking of forks and knives mixing with the soft sounds of satisfied eating. The chicken was tender, the skin perfectly crisped with a blend of herbs that Daisy had somehow managed to infuse just right. The mashed potatoes were creamy, with a hint of garlic and butter that melted on the tongue, and the roasted vegetables — carrots, green beans, and zucchini — were seasoned with just enough salt and pepper to enhance their natural sweetness.

"This chicken is incredible," Brooke said after taking a bite, her eyes widening in surprise. "Seriously, Daisy, what's your secret?"

Daisy grinned, brushing a stray blonde lock behind her ear. "Oh, you know, just a little love and a whole lot of butter."

Cody, halfway through his drumstick, piped up with his mouth full. "It's the best chicken ever!"

"Hey now, don't talk with your mouth full," I gently reminded him, though I couldn't help but smile at his enthusiasm.

Caroline spoke up then, her voice soft but warm. "Daisy's right, though. Butter makes everything better. But there's something about cooking at home that just… it makes the food taste better, you know?"

Brooke nodded, smiling. "I think you're right. Maybe I've been spending too much time eating out or takeaway. This feels… better. More real."

Daisy's face lit up, clearly pleased. "Well, if you ever need a home-cooked meal, you know where to find us."

"Careful," Brooke teased, "I might take you up on that."

"So, Cody," Daisy said, breaking the gentle silence, "you've been explorin' outside already, huh? Did you find Tink?"

"Yeah!" Cody exclaimed, brightening immediately. "She was chasing something, but I don't know what it was. We ran around the field for a while, and then she found a stick, and we played fetch."

"She probably chased off some squirrels," I said, chuckling. "Tink's always after something."

Cody nodded eagerly, clearly delighted with his afternoon adventure. "Can I go play with her after dinner?"

Brooke shot me a questioning glance, and I gave

her a reassuring smile. “Sure, buddy. Just be careful and don’t go too far, alright? Always within earshot.”

“Okay, Dad!” Cody said, finishing off the last of his drumstick before diving into the mashed potatoes.

Caroline leaned forward slightly, smiling at Cody’s enthusiasm. “You really like it out here, don’t you?”

Cody nodded, his mouth full of food. After swallowing, he said, “Yeah, it’s way better than home. There’s so much space to run around, and Tink’s here. And I like being with Dad.”

My heart swelled at that, and I couldn’t help but reach over to ruffle his hair. “I like having you here too, buddy.”

Brooke watched the exchange with a soft smile, her hand resting on her mug of water. “It’s good for him to be here. I can see how happy he is.”

Daisy leaned in with a mischievous grin. “Well, I reckon if Cody’s gonna stick around more, we’ll have to put him to work on the farm. Maybe teach him how to milk the cows.”

Cody’s eyes went wide. “Really?”

"Sure!" Daisy laughed. "You can't hang around here all the time and do nothin' now, can you? A boy needs to learn a trade."

Cody beamed, and Brooke chuckled. "Sounds like something Cody will love."

Caroline nodded in agreement. "And he can drop by the library when he's in the mood for books."

"Oh, I love reading!" Cody said.

Brooke's gaze shifted between Caroline and Daisy, and I could see her taking them both in — these two women who had become such a big part of my life. There was curiosity in her eyes, but also something warmer.

"So, how did you two meet Sean?" Brooke asked, her tone casual but genuinely interested. Her gaze was on Caroline, inviting her to speak first.

Caroline hesitated for a moment, her cheeks coloring slightly before she spoke. "Well, I helped him with the... with the magic stuff when he first came to town, so..." Her voice trailed off a little, some of her shyness resurfacing.

Daisy, ever the extrovert, jumped in with a grin,

saving her harem sister. "Sean and I are neighbors." She winked at me, her blue eyes twinkling with mischief. "I came to borrow a cup of sugar, and we've been thick as thieves ever since."

I laughed, shaking my head at her antics. Brooke joined in. "Sounds like you've both been keeping him good company," she said, looking between them again. She knew something was up here, and she seemed interested to find out more.

I was pretty sure that she would. I smirked, leaning back in my chair. "What can I say? I'm lucky."

The conversation flowed easily from there, the atmosphere growing even warmer as Brooke and the girls shared stories about their lives, their experiences, and their hopes for the future. Cody, full from the meal, leaned against me, sleepy but content, while the chatter around the table continued.

Chapter 17

After dinner, Brooke and I stepped onto the porch, carrying two mugs of freshly brewed coffee. The sky had begun to darken. Cody was playing inside with Tink and Daisy and Caroline, the sound of his laughter drifting out through the open window.

Brooke cradled her mug between her hands,

taking a deep breath and exhaling slowly as we sat down on the steps. I glanced over at her, admiring the way the fading light touched her face, softening her features.

"This is nice," she said, her voice low and relaxed. "The quiet… the air."

I smiled, nodding. "Yeah, it's peaceful out here. It's part of why I love it. No distractions, just life as it is."

She took a sip of her coffee, then glanced back toward the house, where Cody's laughter rang out again. "I appreciate what you've done, Sean," she said quietly, her voice growing more serious. "The way you've been handling everything… it's been good for him. And for me too, if I'm honest."

I turned toward her slightly, giving her my full attention. "I'm just doing what feels right," I said, watching her closely. "For Cody. And for you."

Brooke shifted her weight, turning toward me a bit more as well. Her eyes met mine, searching for something, her expression thoughtful. "I've been thinking about what you showed me — the magic. It's… well, I'm still processing it, but it's kind of wondrous, you know? A little scary, maybe, but also exciting. It makes me think about how much I don't know about the world anymore. It's like it opened a door to something I never thought was real."

Hearing her speak about the magic like that made my chest tighten with a mix of relief and hope. This was a big step, her acknowledging that excitement along with the fear.

"I get that," I said, keeping my tone calm and reassuring. "It's a lot to take in. When I first started to figure out what I could do, it was overwhelming. But after a while… you get used to it. It starts to feel natural. Like it was always there, waiting to be discovered."

She nodded slowly, biting her lip for a moment. "I think that's part of what intrigues me," she admitted. "It's this whole other side of you — of everything — that I never knew existed. And now that I do… I can't help but feel curious about it."

Encouraged by her words, I leaned forward slightly, resting my forearms on my knees. "There's a lot more to it than what I showed you," I said. "I've learned a lot since you last visited, and Daisy and Caroline have been helping me explore it all. We even went on an expedition recently… something that showed us just how real the dangers out there are."

Her brow furrowed with interest. "An expedition? What kind of danger are you talking about?"

I smiled faintly, knowing this was going to sound like a wild tale, but the glimmer of excitement in her eyes told me she was ready to hear it.

"There's a place called Harrwick," I began. "A realm we traveled to through a magical portal. We arrived in a ruined village. It had been destroyed by a troll, a massive one. We set traps, worked together, and eventually took it down."

Brooke's eyes widened, her lips parting slightly in disbelief. "A troll?" she echoed, her voice tinged with awe.

I nodded, grinning a little now. "Yeah. It was no small task, believe me. We had to be smart about it — set traps, use every bit of magic and skill we had. But we did it. And I won't lie… it felt good. Dangerous, sure, but there's something about facing down a creature like that and coming out on top."

She shook her head slowly, processing what I was telling her. "I can't even imagine… It's like something out of a movie!"

"Yeah, that's what it feels like sometimes," I admitted. "But it's real. And now that I'm beginning to understand how the magic works, I'm learning more about what I can do with it. There's still a lot to figure out, but it's helping me protect the people I care about. That's what matters."

Brooke's gaze softened as she looked at me, her fingers lightly tapping the rim of her coffee mug. "I can see that," she said quietly. "I think that's what excites me the most about all this… knowing that you have this power and you're using it to protect us. It makes me feel… safe."

I reached over, resting a hand gently on her knee. "That's what I want, Brooke. For you and Cody to feel safe here. To know that no matter what, I'll be ready."

She smiled at that, her eyes holding mine for a long moment. "You're doing a good job of it, Sean. And… I'm glad I'm here. I'm glad I can see it for myself."

I squeezed her knee softly, feeling a surge of warmth spread through me. "Me too, Brooke. I've missed this… having you close."

She smiled, her eyes shimmering a little in the soft evening light, and I could tell she felt the same.

I took a sip of my coffee, enjoying the easy silence that settled between us. When I looked over at Brooke, there was something else in her eyes — a question, unspoken but hanging there, waiting. After a moment, she turned to face me fully.

"Sean…" she began softly, her voice tentative. "There's something I've been wondering about."

I met her gaze, giving her my full attention. "What's on your mind?"

Brooke hesitated, her fingers tracing the rim of her coffee mug. She glanced toward the house again, where Daisy and Caroline were still inside with Cody.

"It's about Daisy and Caroline," she said finally. "I can tell there's more going on with them… with all of you. I mean, the way they look at you, the way they act around you. It's pretty clear it's not *just* friendship."

I nodded, knowing this conversation was inevitable. I had to be open with her — Brooke deserved that, and more importantly, this was part of my life now. "You're right," I said, my voice calm. "Daisy and Caroline aren't just friends. They're my girlfriends — both of them."

Brooke blinked, clearly trying to process what I'd just said. Her eyebrows lifted slightly in surprise, but there wasn't any immediate judgment in her eyes — just curiosity. "So… you're with both of them? At the same time?"

I nodded, setting my coffee down on the porch beside me. "Yeah. We're in a relationship — a serious one. It's not just casual. I love both of them, and they love me."

For a moment, Brooke just stared at me, processing everything. Then, she let out a soft laugh, shaking her head. "Wow. That's… I mean, it's definitely not what I expected to hear." She glanced back toward the house. "And they're both okay with this? Sharing you with each other?"

"They are," I said. "We've talked it through, laid

everything out. It's not something we rushed into. Daisy and Caroline… they care about each other too. It's more than just them being okay with it. We all make this work together."

Brooke tucked a strand of black hair behind her ear as she processed what I'd said. "You love them both?" she asked quietly, her voice tinged with something I couldn't quite place.

"I do," I replied without hesitation. "I love them both, and they both love me. I know it's not traditional, but it feels right."

Brooke took a sip of her coffee, her gaze thoughtful. "You know… it's funny. Back when we were together, we had our own fun, explored things a little." She shot me a look that carried a hint of mischief. "But *this* is different."

I chuckled softly, remembering some crazy nights. "Yeah, we did have our fun," I admitted, smiling at the memory. "But this… this isn't just experimenting. It's a relationship. We're all committed to each other, emotionally and physically."

Brooke nodded slowly, her eyes still distant, as if she were piecing something together. "So, they both live here with you?"

"They've been staying over a lot lately," I said. "Daisy has her farm, so she still spends some time there, but we're together a lot. It's becoming something like a family." I nodded firmly. "Which is what I want, honestly."

She leaned back a little, her gaze flicking over me, curious and thoughtful. "And that works? No jealousy, no problems?"

"There's always challenges," I said honestly. "No relationship is perfect. But we talk. We're open with each other. If something comes up, we deal with it."

Brooke went quiet for a moment, sipping her coffee again. Her expression was thoughtful, her eyes narrowing slightly as if she were wrestling with something.

I could see she was working things out, and I let her — at her own speed. I sat beside her silently and sipped my coffee, waiting for the next question to come. Even though I could already guess what it was going to be.

Finally, she let out a slow breath. "And what about me?" she asked softly, her voice barely above a whisper. “Where do I fit into all of this?”

“It doesn’t change how I feel about you, Brooke. That part’s the same. I’ve never stopped loving you, and I won’t. But Daisy and Caroline… they’re part of my life now. I care about them deeply, and I’m not going to send them away.”

Brooke nodded, her expression understanding, even as she absorbed the weight of my words. “I wouldn’t ask you to,” she said quietly, her eyes lifting to meet mine. “I’m not here to disrupt what you’ve built with them. It’s just… a lot to take in, you know? But weirdly enough, I don’t feel like I need to compete with them or anything. I don’t feel… jealous.”

That caught my attention. I tilted my head, studying her face, and saw the truth in her eyes. “You don’t feel jealous?”

She shook her head, a small, almost amused smile tugging at the corners of her lips. “No, not at all. It’s weird, right? I thought I would. I thought the idea of you being with other women would make me feel… territorial or something. But it doesn’t. If anything, I’m… I don’t know, *happy,* maybe? Like you’ve found people who care about you and want to be with you. It doesn't feel threatening."

I couldn't help but smile at that. "It's not weird at all, Brooke. You're not losing anything. What we had was always real, and what we could have again could be just as real. The girls don't change that."

Brooke let out a small laugh, shaking her head. "I guess not. And honestly, seeing how happy Cody is around them… it's nice. He really likes them, doesn't he?"

"He does," I said with a grin. "Daisy and Caroline are great with him. It's like he feels right at home with them."

Her smile softened. "That's what makes this easier, I think. Seeing him happy. I know you'll always take care of him, Sean, but it's good to see him connecting with Daisy and Caroline too. It feels… like it's right."

I nodded, feeling the same sense of ease settle over me. "It *is* right. And if you ever feel like you want to be part of that, you'll always have a place here, Brooke. You and Cody both."

Brooke turned to me then, her blue eyes bright

with something new — something hopeful. "You think so? You think I could… I could fit?"

I turned to her, meeting her gaze head-on. "Honestly, Brooke, if you're asking *me* — if you want to know what I want — well, I want you to be part of this too. You and Cody. I've never stopped loving you, and I never will. We've been through so much together, and I still believe we can make something work. It might look different than before, but that doesn't mean it can't be good."

Brooke swallowed, her blue eyes flicking down to the porch for a moment before she looked back at me. "You really think so? I mean… I don't know if I can just jump into something like that. It's a lot to wrap my head around."

"I'm not asking you to jump into anything," I said gently. "I'm asking you to take your time, to figure out what feels right for you. You don't have to make any decisions now. But if there's a part of you that's curious, if there's something about this that interests you… then I'm here, Brooke. We all are."

Brooke let out a shaky breath, her fingers

tightening around her coffee mug. "It's just so... *different*. I never thought I'd be sitting here, talking about being part of something like this. But..." She trailed off, biting her lip as if debating whether to say what was on her mind.

"But what?" I asked softly, leaning a little closer to her.

She glanced at me, her eyes filled with a mix of confusion and something else — something that looked a lot like interest. "But maybe... maybe it's not as crazy as I thought. Maybe... there's something about it that makes sense." She paused, then added, almost shyly, "I've always been open-minded, you know that. And maybe... I don't know, maybe I could explore this. See what it's like."

A spark of hope ignited in my chest. I reached over, taking her hand gently. "You don't have to decide now, Brooke. But if you're willing to see where this could go, then I'd love that. I think we could build something really special, all of us together."

Brooke smiled softly, squeezing my hand. "I never thought I'd be considering something like this. But with you… maybe it's worth seeing where it leads."

I smiled, my heart lightening at her words. "Think about this," I said. "We're not in a hurry, okay?"

Brooke nodded, her eyes meeting mine with a glimmer of something new — something that hinted at possibilities I hadn't dared hope for. "Yeah," she agreed softly before squeezing my hand. "We're not. Thanks, Sean."

For a while longer, we sat in a comfortable silence on the porch. The air was still, save for the occasional rustle of leaves in the breeze. I could hear Cody laughing with Tink and Caroline and Daisy inside. It would be his bedtime soon.

Brooke took a slow, deep breath, and I could see the tension slipping from her shoulders. She turned her head toward me, a small, contented smile on her lips.

"You know," she said softly, "I feel… happier right now than I have in a long time."

I turned to face her fully, watching as she gazed out at the yard, her expression peaceful. "I'm glad," I said. "It feels good having you here,

Brooke. Like things are falling into place."

Her eyes met mine, and for a moment, there was something familiar between us — something unspoken that I'd missed. That connection that had always been there, even after all we'd been through.

Without thinking, I leaned in, closing the space between us.

And then, I kissed her.

It was soft, tentative at first — just a brush of the lips. But the moment we connected, everything else fell away. All the memories, all the feelings we'd shared before rushed back, and for a brief, perfect moment, it felt like nothing had changed. Her lips were warm and familiar, and I felt her respond, kissing me back with the same gentle intensity.

When we pulled away, her blue eyes fluttered open, and there was a hint of surprise mixed with something deeper in her gaze. She let out a soft breath, her lips curving into a smile.

"I liked that," she whispered, her voice almost hesitant. Then, she reached up, brushing her fingers lightly over her lips as if still feeling the warmth of the kiss. “But… we should take it slow, okay?”

I nodded, my heart still racing from the kiss. “Yeah. Slow is good.”

She smiled again, her eyes holding mine for a moment longer before we both settled back into that comfortable silence, and I knew the first steps had been taken.

Chapter 18

After our time together on the porch, Brooke and I walked back into the house to find Cody sitting on the floor, completely absorbed in playing with Tink. He was laughing and tossing a ball for her to fetch, the dog's excitement nearly matching his own. Daisy and Caroline sat nearby, smiling as they watched the two play.

I crouched down beside Cody, gently ruffling his hair. "Hey, buddy," I said, my voice soft. "Time to start winding down. How about we get you ready for bed?"

Cody glanced up at me, his face lit with that typical reluctance. "Already?" he asked, but there was no real protest in his voice.

I nodded. "Yeah, it's been a long day, and you've got plenty of time tomorrow to play with Tink. Plus, I want to make sure you're all rested for whatever fun we get into."

He sighed dramatically but smiled and stood up. "Okay, Dad. Will I sleep in the guest room with Mom tonight?"

"Yeah," I said, gesturing for him to follow me. "Let's go get you tucked in."

The guest room was already set up, with fresh linens and soft pillows. As Cody climbed into bed, I tucked the blankets around him, smoothing them out over his small frame.

"You comfortable?" I asked, sitting on the edge of the bed.

Cody nodded, yawning as he nestled into the pillow. "Yeah, it's perfect."

I smiled and leaned down, pressing a kiss to his forehead. "Goodnight, buddy. I'll be just downstairs if you need anything, okay?"

"Goodnight, Dad," he murmured, his eyes already half-closed. Tink settled at the foot of the bed, curling up to sleep next to him. With one last glance to make sure he was settled, I quietly left the room, closing the door halfway behind me.

I headed back downstairs, where the girls were seated at the coffee table, their voices low and comfortable. Brooke looked relaxed, but I noticed the subtle glances Daisy was giving me, a playful glint in her eyes. She had a way of lightening any mood, and I could sense she was about to do just that.

I grabbed a seat beside Daisy on the couch, and she leaned in, her lips curving into a teasing smile. "So, how's the little man doin'? All snuggled up?"

"Out like a light," I replied, returning her smile. "He's had a full day."

Daisy chuckled softly, leaning back. "Can't blame him. Tink probably wore him out good." She took a sip of her drink, her eyes glinting with a bit of that playful energy she always had.

Caroline nodded, glancing up from where she was tracing her finger along the rim of her glass. "He seems really happy here, Sean. It's... nice to see."

I smiled. "It's good to have him here. I miss him when he's not around. Having the house full like this... it feels right."

Daisy's gaze flicked to me, and there was a softer edge to her smile this time. "Reckon it does," she hummed, her voice casual but carrying a hint of something else. She reached over and rested her hand lightly on my arm.

The touch was intimate, and I noticed from the little light in her blue eyes that her mind was drifting to other activities. She was insatiable like that, and I loved it.

Caroline gave a small, knowing smile, fully aware of where her harem sister's interests were moving.

And so was Brooke. A slight — and rare — blush colored her cheeks as she had been following our exchange quietly. She cleared her throat, set her glass down, and stretched her arms above her head with a yawn. "Well, you've definitely got a lot to be proud of, Sean," she said, standing up and giving me a soft smile. "But I think it's time for me to turn in. I'm ready to crash after today."

As she spoke, Daisy snuggled closer to me, her hand on the inside of my thigh. I returned Brooke's smile. "Glad you feel that way. Sleep well, Brooke. I'll see you in the morning."

She smiled warmly at Daisy and Caroline. "Goodnight, you two. Thanks again for the dinner — it was amazing."

Caroline nodded shyly. "Goodnight, Brooke."

"Sleep tight," Daisy added with a wink. "We'll be up in... well, in a bit..."

Brooke gave a soft laugh before heading up the stairs, leaving the three of us alone in the cozy warmth of the kitchen.

The room grew quieter, the distant sounds of the forest filtering in through the open window. I settled back down in my chair, feeling the weight of the day finally starting to catch up to me, though Daisy's playful energy lingered, as did her soft hand on my thigh.

"You know," Daisy said, her voice dropping just

a little, though still light and teasing, "I think Brooke's startin' to get real comfortable with all of us. I reckon that's a good sign."

Caroline smiled softly, nodding in agreement. "It's obvious she trusts you, Sean."

I leaned back, resting my arm on the back of the couch, letting Daisy snuggle even closer. "Yeah, it feels like she's starting to see what we have here. I'm just glad she's giving it a chance."

Daisy smiled, glancing up at me with a hint of mischief in her eyes. "Well, if she sticks around long enough... she might just start enjoyin' things as much as we do."

Caroline blushed, but she didn't look away, her gaze steady on mine. "I think... she could," she agreed softly, her voice warm but cautious, like she was feeling out the possibilities.

I chuckled, sensing the shift in the air but keeping things light. "We'll see where it goes. No need to rush."

Daisy grinned and leaned her head against my shoulder, her tone playful. "Yeah... no need to rush, but I'm thinkin' we've got something good going here, don't we?"

I smiled, wrapping my arm around her. "Yeah, we do."

Chapter 19

I sank into the plush couch, the warmth of Daisy's body pressed against mine. Her light summer dress rustled softly as she snuggled closer to me, her blonde hair tickling my cheek.

"You know, I think Brooke is real nice an' pretty," she said, her blue eyes earnest and wide.

Caroline looked up. "Oh, I agree," she said.

"Brooke is *very* pretty. I can understand why you married her, Sean."

"She is," I agreed. "But she's not just pretty. Brooke is intelligent, passionate, and a good mother too."

The admiration in Caroline's and Daisy's eyes was unmistakable as they listened to my words. Caroline tucked a strand of red hair behind her ear as she listened, and Daisy nodded softly.

"It's really nice to hear you talk about her like that," Caroline said softly. "It's obvious you still care."

"Yup, yup, that's for sure," Daisy chimed in, resting her head on my shoulder. Then, she playfully nudged me. "All I'm gonna say is she couldn't have been *that* smart, seein' as she let you go and all."

"Hey, now," Caroline scolded gently, giving Daisy a pointed look. "I don't think they broke up because they didn't love each other."

My eyebrows shot up in surprise at her comment. She was right, but I wondered how she knew. "Oh? What makes you say that?" I asked, genuinely curious about her perspective.

"Uh, well," Caroline began, her cheeks flushing a soft pink. "I'm sure Brooke still loves you. I can... I can see it in her eyes when she looks at you."

Daisy nodded, her blue eyes serious as she met my gaze. "Yeah, I reckon Caroline's right about that."

As the revelation hung in the air, I wondered how their observations made them feel. "Doesn't that bother either of you?" I asked, searching their faces for any signs of discomfort or jealousy.

In response, Caroline rose from her chair and gracefully settled herself on the couch beside me, her body close to mine. Her green eyes held nothing but warmth and affection as she looked at me. "Not at all, Sean. I love sharing you."

"Same here," Daisy chimed in, her hand resting on my knee. "You know my story, Sean. I don't get jealous quick."

She then shot me a lopsided grin as she placed her hand on my groin and bit her lip. "Besides," she drawled with a playful grin, "there's more than enough of you to share with Brooke too."

Caroline giggled in agreement, her green eyes sparkling with delight. "She's right," she purred.

I laughed and reached over, wanting to pinch Daisy's side, but the playful little blonde was quick and twisted her shapely torso so that my hand poked her firm breast instead. She was not wearing a bra underneath.

"Oops," she purred as I poked the soft flesh, shooting me a challenging look.

I chuckled as I moved my hand over the soft curvature until my fingers came to where her nipple was poking against the fabric, and I squeezed it gently through the thin material of her summer dress.

"Ooh…" Daisy bit her lip, her eyes darkening with lust. "You're pushin' my buttons, baby."

"Oh my," I teased. "I'd better stop, then!"

"Oh no, you don't!" she hummed as she leaned in for a kiss, her soft lips meeting mine. As our tongues tangled, I heard Caroline giggle, then felt her hand join Daisy's on my groin. I groaned at the pleasurable touch, raising my pelvis to meet their hands.

My cock hardened under their ministrations, and I broke the kiss with Daisy to turn my attention to Caroline. Her cheeks were flushed, and she looked at me with lustful green eyes. With a hungry gaze, I captured her lips with mine, tasting the sweet warmth of her mouth.

As our passion grew, my hands found their way to Caroline's full breasts, squeezing them gently through her crop top. The feel of her soft flesh beneath the fabric was a delight, and I reveled in the moans that escaped her throat as we kissed.

A moment later, she pulled away from our kiss with a mischievous glint in her eyes. It was as if a switch had been flipped inside her, transforming the normally reserved librarian into a wild creature of desire.

"Uh, I think it's time for this to come off," she murmured, her fingers deftly unhooking her crop top and slipping it over her head.

Her freckled breasts spilled out, full and heavy, their rosy nipples already hard with arousal. Before I could even catch my breath, Caroline leaned in to capture my lips once more, her tongue eagerly exploring my mouth.

All the while, Daisy continued to massage my throbbing cock through my pants, her skilled fingers sending shivers of pleasure up my spine. I groaned into Caroline's mouth as I reached out blindly, my hand finding one of Daisy's firm breasts and giving it a gentle squeeze.

"Looks like you got your hands full there, Sean," Daisy teased, her voice low and sultry. "But I got more for you."

With a playful wink, Daisy peeled off her summer dress, revealing her curvaceous body clad in nothing but a pink thong. She crawled forward on the couch, her tight ass high in the air as she worked on unbuttoning my pants.

"Damn," Daisy murmured appreciatively as my cock sprang free, already hard and straining for attention. "You sure know how to make a girl feel welcome, darlin'."

I grinned, one eye on Daisy's pretty butt as Caroline and I continued to kiss passionately, my free hand now roaming over her soft, freckled flesh as I explored every inch of her voluptuous form.

"Suck it, Daisy," Caroline muttered around our kiss at Daisy, watching her as she handled my cock.

Daisy licked her lips and leaned closer.

The moment Daisy's warm, wet mouth enveloped my cock, I felt a bolt of pleasure shoot through my entire body. Caroline's lips were still locked onto mine as I groaned into her mouth, my hands instinctively gravitating toward her large, freckled breasts, kneading them gently as I felt Daisy's eager tongue swirling around the head of my shaft.

"Damn, Daisy..." I panted, breaking away from Caroline's kiss just long enough to express my appreciation for her harem sister's skillful ministrations.

My eyes turned back to Caroline, and I saw her lusty, wide eyes. I wanted to taste her – *needed* to taste her.

"Caroline," I said. "Stand up. Come here and let me lick your pussy."

Her cheeks flushed crimson at my request, but she couldn't hide the lustful gleam in her eyes as she complied. Lifting her skirt, she revealed her cute lace panties and peeled them down her shapely legs before stepping out of them and tossing them aside. She then stood on the couch, her trembling thighs bracketing my face as she lowered her pussy to meet my eager mouth.

The taste of Caroline was divine, and I teased her folds and her swollen little nub with my tongue, each delicious stroke causing her moans of pleasure to grow louder and more urgent. Every lick, every flick, every tantalizing tease brought her closer to the edge, and I reveled in the knowledge that I held the power to push her over it.

"Sean," Caroline whimpered, her voice little more than a breathless plea as she clung to my shoulders for support. "Oh, God... don't stop... please, don't stop..."

As my tongue continued to explore the depths of Caroline's quivering pussy, I felt Daisy's talented mouth working in tandem with her skilled hands, coaxing me ever closer to the brink of ecstasy. It was maddeningly delicious, and I felt my power gather for a release.

My world narrowed until all that existed were the intoxicating flavors and sensations coursing through me — the heat of Caroline's sex against my lips, the rhythmic suction of Daisy's mouth on my cock, and the breathless sighs of pleasure from both women as they reveled in the blissful union of our shared passion.

As I continued to devour Caroline's sweetness, I felt her body tense and her legs tremble. "Sean... oh, my God, I'm gonna cum," Caroline cried out, her voice barely a whisper as she clutched my head tighter.

Just then, in the corner of my vision, I noticed a familiar figure lurking near the stairway.

It was Brooke.

She wore one of my old button-down shirts, which hung open to reveal her full breasts. Her eyes were closed, one hand massaging a breast while the other had slipped beneath her panties. She was completely lost in her lustful voyeurism.

God, that was hot…

A wicked grin spread across my face, but I didn't make it known that I saw her. Instead, I focused back on Caroline, who shuddered and cried out as her orgasm washed over her. She collapsed onto the couch, her body still quivering from the aftershocks of her climax.

"God, Sean," Caroline panted, "that was amazing."

I gave her a grin, my thoughts already drifting to what I would do next. "Daisy, come up here," I commanded gently.

She eagerly obliged, releasing my cock from her mouth with a wet pop. As she clambered onto the couch beside me, I turned her around so that she was on her hands and knees, her sumptuous ass facing me in its pretty thong.

"Oh yes, Sean," she purred, throwing her head back in anticipation of what was coming.

I smiled and came up behind her, giving her pretty ass a smack as my eyes flicked over to where Brooke remained hidden, watching us intently.

I pulled aside Daisy's thong and gave her round ass a firm slap with my cock, eliciting a delighted moan from her.

"Yes," Caroline moaned from behind me, still recovering from her orgasm. "Take her, Sean."

Fired on by her words, and knowing that Brooke was watching, I pushed my throbbing length into Daisy's warm, inviting depths.

"Ah, Sean... yes!" she cried out, her body welcoming me.

Soft mewls of lust from Daisy filled the room as I thrust into her from behind. Her body yielded to my every movement, the gentle sway of her hips inviting me deeper.

"Pull my hair, Sean, please," she begged.

I gathered a handful of her blonde locks in my grip. As I pulled on her hair, Daisy let out a delicious moan and pushed back against me, urging me to fuck her faster, her firm ass jiggling in her thong. I happily complied, driving my cock into her wet warmth with increasing speed and force.

With each deep thrust, Daisy's ass jiggled enticingly before me. Caroline, not wanting to be left out, came up behind me and pressed herself against my back. Her breasts nestled against my skin, while her hands roamed over my chest, sending shivers down my spine.

"It looks so beautiful," she whispered into my ear, her breath hot and inviting. My mind raced with the sensation of their bodies, and the knowledge that Brooke was watching us — hidden yet so close, pleasuring herself to our passionate display.

Daisy's tight, slick heat enveloped me as I continued to fuck her from behind, the pressure building within me. The sensation of her curves bouncing against me, the sound of her throaty moans, and the feel of Caroline's hands wandering over my body all blended together into a symphony of pleasure that threatened to bring me to the edge.

"Sean, I can tell you're getting close," Caroline murmured, her fingers teasingly caressing my balls. "Let me help you get there."

"Please do," I gasped, the pleasure intensifying with each stroke.

In that moment, as Brooke's trembling form caught my eye, I reveled in the knowledge that she was getting off on seeing us together. My orgasm drew nearer with each thrust, an irresistible force pulling me closer and closer to the edge.

Daisy's cries of pleasure grew louder and more intense, her nails digging into the couch cushions. I could feel the powerful waves of her orgasm crashing through her body as she tightened around me, gripping my cock with an almost desperate fervor.

"Sean... Oh God, Sean!" she moaned, her voice breaking with the intensity of her release. Her body quivered beneath me, her ass jiggling against my hips.

"Please, baby… Ahhh… Cum all over me," Daisy begged, her eyes wild with lust as she looked at me over her shoulder. "Cover my ass in your hot cum!"

"Go on, Sean," Caroline hummed "Give her what she's begging for."

As I looked down at Daisy, her flushed skin slick with sweat and passion, I knew I couldn't hold back any longer. The sight of her writhing in ecstasy, combined with Caroline's whispered encouragements and the knowledge that Brooke was so close by, brought me to the brink.

"Here it comes, baby," I warned, pulling out just in time.

My orgasm hit me like a tidal wave, sending thick ropes of cum splattering across Daisy's quivering cheeks, her thong, and her slender back.

"Oh, yeah! Make me feel like a good girl, Sean," she purred, arching her back to receive every last drop. "I want it all."

"Look at you," Caroline murmured, admiration clear in her voice as she watched Daisy's display. "Such a beautiful mess."

Breathless, I gave Daisy's cum-slicked ass a playful slap, causing her to yelp and giggle.

It was then that I caught a glimpse of Brooke, still trembling from her own orgasm as she quickly turned to slip up the stairs. The sight of her, so overcome by what she'd witnessed, only added to the thrill of our passionate encounter.

I grinned and sunk back on the couch. "Oof," I muttered. "That was good."

"It sure was, baby," Daisy hummed, then laughed. "I need a towel, though!"

The three of us, spent and satisfied, sat nestled together on the couch as our laughter filled the room. I could still feel the warmth of their bodies pressed against me, Daisy to my left and Caroline to my right, each with a satisfied smile painted across their beautiful faces.

"You two sure know how to make a man feel good," I said, my voice tinged with amusement and pleasure. "I can't remember the last time I felt this... alive."

"Well," Daisy hummed, her blue eyes sparkling, "ain't nothin' like some good lovin' to get the blood pumpin'." She snuggled closer, burying her face in my chest, and I couldn't help but chuckle.

"Yeah," Caroline agreed, her cheeks still flushed. She tucked a lock of red hair behind her ear, and I caught a glimpse of that familiar shy smile before she leaned in for a lingering kiss.

My mind raced with thoughts of what had just happened. Brooke had come and watched us… And she had obviously liked what she had seen.

A smile settled on my face as I pulled the girls in and settled back. This was an interesting development — one that promised a lot of good…

Chapter 20 (Brooke)

Brooke sat on the porch steps, the morning sun warming her skin as she watched Sean and Cody walk toward the nearby lake, fishing rods slung over their shoulders.

It was going to be a father-and-son day. The two of them, fishing by the lake. And Sean — in wholly characteristic fashion — had insisted that they would hike to the lake and not take the car. He was bent on teaching Cody how to pack for a hike and how to travel by foot, and it was a good thing. Cody needed that. He loved it.

Cody's excited chatter floated back to Brooke as she sat there, and she smiled. The simple joy of seeing her son so happy eased some of the tension that had lingered since their arrival. She had been nervous, and the fact that Sean had seemed so calm had made her a little more nervous.

She'd had the feeling like she was coming into this new thing of his, this outdoor life thing that she had rejected, and she had feared he would resent her for not coming along in the first place. But he hadn't, and he still didn't.

It was like he *knew* she had to try life in the city.

Maybe he knew her better than she did.

She took a deep breath, the fresh air a welcome change from the stale city streets she'd grown accustomed to. It felt good here, quiet, peaceful. Sean's house — *their* house, in a way — was full of warmth, laughter, and an ease she hadn't realized she missed so much.

Her thoughts drifted back to last night. After

heading upstairs, she hadn't been able to fall asleep right away, knowing what was happening downstairs. The soft murmurs, the quiet laughter that had followed her up the stairs, and the unmistakable sounds of pleasure...

She'd found herself lingering at the edge of the moment, watching them — Daisy, Caroline, and Sean — come together in a way that was intimate, comfortable, and surprisingly natural.

It had also been *extremely hot* to see Sean claim these beautiful, young women with their blessed, fertile bodies. She hadn't touched herself in a long time — life as a lawyer had her stressed out — but she hadn't been able to help herself, watching Sean claim these willing and submissive women. Seeing him like that, in charge and strong and potent… well, it was like an aphrodisiac. She had climaxed hard, fantasizing about being with them…

And emotionally, it wasn't jealousy she felt. It was something else — curiosity, maybe even admiration for the way they fit together so seamlessly. It left her wondering if there was room for her in this life.

Part of her already knew the answer. Sean was clear enough.

The creak of the porch door drew her attention, and she turned to see Daisy and Caroline stepping outside, both dressed in comfortable hiking clothes. Daisy gave her a broad smile, hands on her hips. "Thought we'd find you out here. Sean said he's taking Cody fishing, so we figured we could head out for a little hike. Thought you might wanna join us?"

Brooke returned the smile, standing up and brushing her hands over her jeans. "That sounds great, actually. I've been cooped up in the city for too long — could use some fresh air."

"Perfect," Daisy said. "There's a great trail not too far from here. Let's head out."

Brooke shot the girls a warm smile. She was thankful for this — for this invitation. Like the meal and the conversation yesterday, it showed her that the girls were open to having her here. It showed her that she wasn't intruding.

They set out along the trail together. At first, they were silent, but Daisy soon enough broke the ice, talking about her childhood memories growing up here in Waycross. She knew the area well, and so did Caroline. Despite her bookishness, the redhead seemed to be at home in nature. She had a deep love for hiking.

As the three of them walked along the path, the conversation flowed easily, helped by Daisy's naturally extroverted nature. Brooke found herself opening up in a way she hadn't expected, sharing stories about her work as a lawyer — how stressful it had become, how she felt like she was constantly fighting a losing battle.

"Sometimes I wonder if it's even worth it," Brooke admitted, kicking a loose stone off the trail. "All the late nights, the pressure... it's exhausting. I don't even know if I enjoy it anymore."

"It sounds rough," Caroline sympathized.

Daisy, ever candid, glanced at her with a knowing smile. "Then quit."

Brooke blinked, surprised by the bluntness. "Quit? Just like that?"

Daisy shrugged. "If it's makin' you miserable, why stick with it? You're smart, capable — there are a million other things you could do. Reckon life's too short to spend it doin' somethin' you hate, ain't it?"

Caroline nodded in agreement. "Daisy's right. You don't have to stay stuck in a job just because it's what you've always done. There's always another path."

Brooke thought about that for a moment, considering the freedom that might come with walking away from the corporate grind. "I guess I've just been afraid to let go. It feels like I'd be giving up on something, even if I don't know what that something is anymore."

"Maybe it's not giving up," Daisy said, stepping over a fallen log with ease. "Maybe it's just moving on to somethin' better."

Brooke laughed softly, glancing around at the serene landscape surrounding them. "You've got a point."

The trail opened up to a small clearing, where the sun pierced the canopy, casting shadows across the ground. The three of them paused, taking a moment to appreciate the view.

Brooke felt a sense of peace settle over her, the weight of her work and responsibilities momentarily lifting. She closed her eyes for a moment, letting the sunlight warm her face and the scent of pine fill her senses. For the first time in what felt like ages, she wasn't thinking about deadlines, phone calls, or courtroom arguments.

She was simply here.

"It's beautiful, isn't it?" Caroline said softly, her voice blending into the tranquility of the moment. Out here in nature, the redhead's natural anxiety subsided a little.

Brooke opened her eyes and smiled. "Yeah, it really is. I forgot how good it feels to just be out in nature."

Daisy stretched her arms above her head, rolling her shoulders before planting her hands on her hips. "That's what I love about this place. Out here, you can let go of all the noise and just be. Ain't much that can't be sorted out with a walk in the woods."

Brooke nodded, appreciating the simplicity of that idea.

As they continued along the trail, the conversation shifted to lighter topics, and she found herself getting to know the women better. Caroline, quiet but insightful, shared her love of hiking, explaining how she often found solace in the woods after long days at the library.

"I used to spend hours at the local library as a kid," Brooke mentioned, surprising herself. "I'd get lost in the books, reading about places I never thought I'd go, adventures I'd never take." She smiled and shook her head. "I lost that along the way, somehow..."

"You ever think about picking it back up? The reading?" Caroline asked, glancing over at her. "There's something comforting about diving into a book. No matter how crazy the world gets, there's always a good story waiting for you."

Brooke thought about that. She used to read all the time, back when she had the mental space for it. "Maybe I will," she said with a thoughtful smile. "I could use an escape that's a little more relaxing than legal documents."

Daisy gave her a teasing nudge. "Or you could always come back to the farm with me. We'll put you to work — no stress, just a good day's labor and fresh air."

Brooke laughed. "I'm not sure I'd be much help on a farm!"

Daisy grinned, shrugging. "You'd pick it up quick enough. If you can handle a courtroom, you can handle a few cows."

Brooke laughed, and they continued to walk and talk. The trail dipped and rose, but the pace was leisurely, no one in a hurry to get anywhere.

"You know," Brooke said after a while, "I didn't expect to feel so... *welcome* here. I was worried at first. But this... it feels nice. Being with you both."

Daisy smiled broadly, her blue eyes twinkling in the sunlight. "We like having you around, Brooke. Ain't no need to feel like you don't belong, 'cause you do belong."

Caroline nodded in agreement, a soft smile on her lips. "Yeah, and I'm glad we're getting to know you better. It's nice, having more people around who appreciate the quiet things — like this."

Brooke felt a warmth spread through her chest. She was beginning to understand why Sean had made this place his home. More than that, she was beginning to understand why she wanted to be part of it.

And that felt good.

Chapter 21

I cast my line into the lake, watching the lure plop down in the calm water, ripples fanning out around it. The air was still, save for the occasional breeze that rustled the trees and the soft hum of insects.

Cody sat next to me on the small wooden dock, his feet dangling over the edge as he held his fishing rod with both hands, his little brows furrowed in concentration.

It felt good, being out here with him like this. Just the two of us, fishing by the lake. These were things I wanted to teach him — not just because fishing was a good way to pass the time, but also because it was a form of subsistence. The more a man could care for himself and his loved ones, the better. I wasn't an advocate of getting rid of society — I believed people needed each other — but there was strength and confidence to be found in the ability to provide. I wanted him to feel and to understand that.

"Dad?" Cody's voice broke the peaceful silence and roused me from my thoughts.

I glanced down at him, smiling. "Yeah, buddy?"

He shifted a little, still staring out at the water. "Do you think… do you think we can come out here more? Like, *a lot* more? I really like it here."

I felt a warmth spread through my chest at his words. I had always known how much Cody loved being out in nature, but hearing him say it like that — like he wanted this to be part of his life — made me feel good. Real good.

"Of course we can, Cody," I said, my voice soft but firm. "Whenever you want to come, you just tell me. This place is yours as much as it's mine. We'll have to work out things with school back in the city, but we always manage, don't we?"

Cody smiled, his small hands gripping the fishing rod tighter. "I like it better here than in stinky Louisville. I don't like it there... it's too loud, and there's no Tink or the woods. And it stinks!"

I nodded, understanding exactly what he meant. Apart from my issues with people living too close together, the smell in Louisville could be something of a problem on its own. "I get it," I said. "It's a lot quieter out here. There's more space to run around and play. More freedom."

He looked up at me then, his expression more serious than I expected. "Do you think Mom could come out here too? Like... more often? I miss when we were all together. Like a family."

The words hit me hard, but in a good way. I could tell he'd been thinking about this for a while, and I was happy he felt free to voice his thoughts with me. I wanted to say the right thing, to make sure he knew that no matter what, I was always going to be here for him.

"I hope so, Cody," I said honestly. "I want that too. I want us to spend more time together as a family, all of us. And I think your mom does too. She needs some time to think things over. She moved to the city for her job, and she will need to give that up. If she does so, she will have to come to that decision on her own, okay? There's no point wanting her to move faster."

"But you think she wants to?"

"I believe so, yes."

His eyes brightened a little at that, and he nodded. "It would be fun. We could go fishing and play with Tink, and I could help on the farm like Daisy said."

I chuckled. "Yeah, Daisy would love that. You'd be a natural at helping out on the farm."

Cody grinned, clearly liking the idea, but then he hesitated for a moment. "And… Caroline too? She's really nice. I like her."

I smiled at that, feeling a little proud of how well the girls had connected with him. "Caroline would love to spend more time with you too, buddy. Both Daisy and Caroline care about you a lot. They want to be part of your life, just like I do."

Cody looked thoughtful for a moment, then nodded. "I like them both. They're really nice to me, and they make you happy, Dad. I want them to be around too."

I was proud of him for saying that. He wasn't just thinking about himself — he was thinking about what made all of us happy, including me. That's all I ever wanted from him — to be with us, to want to be with us.

I reached out, ruffling his hair gently. "I'm really glad to hear that, Cody. We'll figure this all out together, okay? You, me, your mom, Daisy, and Caroline… we'll make it work."

He smiled up at me, his eyes shining with that pure, innocent hope only a kid could have. "Yeah… I think we can."

I nodded, feeling a sense of peace settle over me as I looked out at the lake. It was going to take time, and there would be challenges ahead, but everyone wanted to take the same road. To me, that meant we would get where we needed to be.

As Cody and I made our way back from the lake, the smell of something cooking hit us before we even stepped inside the house. It was savory and warm, the kind of smell that made your stomach rumble in anticipation. I grinned, glancing down at my son, who seemed to pick up on the scent too, his nose twitching.

When we reached the porch, I could already hear the sound of laughter drifting out from the open kitchen window. Stepping through the front door, I was greeted by the sight of Brooke, Daisy, and Caroline in the kitchen, all busy with lunch. Brooke stood at the stove, stirring something in a pot, while Daisy hovered over a cutting board, and Caroline chopped vegetables at the counter, her movements precise and careful.

"You're putting way too much pepper in that!" Brooke teased, her tone light and playful.

Daisy shot her a mock glare. "Oh, hush! You've got no sense of flavor if you think this is too much!"

Caroline giggled softly, not looking up from her chopping. "Let her be, Brooke. Daisy's the one in charge of the spices today."

I couldn't help but smile at the easy banter between them. It was the kind of scene I'd always wanted to come home to — laughter, warmth, and the smell of a home-cooked meal. I stepped into the kitchen, Cody right behind me, his face lighting up at the sight of the spread on the counter.

"Smells incredible in here," I said, setting my fishing rod down by the door. "What's on the menu?"

Daisy turned to face me, her blue eyes sparkling with mischief. "Oh, just a little something special. Chicken stew, mashed potatoes, and fresh bread. And don't worry, Brooke's got dessert covered — *if* she doesn't burn it," she added with a wink.

Brooke rolled her eyes, smirking as she stirred the pot. "I've got it under control. I'm not *that* bad."

"You're not great either," I teased, stepping behind her and pressing a quick kiss to her cheek. She swatted me lightly with the spoon, but I saw the smile on her lips.

"You two have a good time?" Caroline asked,

her soft voice drawing my attention. She looked up from the veggies she was chopping, her smile warm and welcoming.

"Yeah, we did," Cody answered for me, bouncing on his toes. "We didn't catch any fish, though."

"You know what they say, buddy," I added, ruffling his hair. "It's not about the catch, it's about the time spent."

Daisy snorted from her spot by the counter. "Isn't that just what people who don't catch anything always say?"

Everyone burst out laughing at that, even Cody, who gave me a playful nudge as if siding with Daisy on this one. I grinned, loving the sound of their laughter filling the house. It felt good, like this was how things were supposed to be.

"So, how long until it's ready?" I asked, eyeing the pot on the stove. The smell was seriously starting to get to me.

"Almost done," Brooke replied, glancing over her shoulder at me. "You two get cleaned up, and we'll set the table."

"On it," I said, giving Cody a gentle push

toward the bathroom. “Go wash up, kiddo.”

As we cleaned up, I could still hear the girls chatting in the kitchen, their voices light and full of energy. When Cody and I came back, the table was already set, and the girls were bringing over the final touches — steaming bowls of mashed potatoes, a pot of chicken stew, and fresh bread that had me practically drooling.

We sat down together, the five of us around the table. Cody, of course, was all energy and excitement, immediately digging into his food with enthusiasm. I couldn’t blame him. The stew was perfect — hearty and rich, the kind of meal that made you feel warm from the inside out.

“This is incredible,” I said after my first bite, glancing at Daisy, who had clearly taken charge of the kitchen. “Seriously, this might be your best meal yet.”

Daisy gave me a mock bow from her seat, grinning ear to ear. “Why, thank you! I’ll be here all week.”

Brooke shook her head with a smile. “It’s amazing, Daisy. And for the record, I wasn’t *too* worried about you overdoing the pepper.”

"Sure you weren't," Daisy quipped, reaching for the bread as she stuck out her tongue. "You city folk can't handle real flavor."

Caroline jumped in. "I think it's perfect," she said, her quiet voice cutting through the playful banter. "Just the right amount of everything."

I shot Caroline a grateful smile, noticing how much more comfortable she seemed today. She wasn't usually one for big group settings, but I could see how much effort she was putting into being part of this. It made me appreciate her even more.

Cody piped up then, his mouth full of mashed potatoes. "Dad, do you think we can go fishing again tomorrow? Maybe we'll catch something this time!"

I laughed, wiping a bit of gravy off his cheek. "Well, tomorrow you and your mom are going home again. You have school. But maybe you can come back real soon, and we'll give it another shot, huh?"

"Maybe you should ask Daisy for some fishing tips," Brooke suggested, her eyes twinkling with amusement. "She seems to be the expert on *everything.*"

Daisy grinned, clearly enjoying the teasing. "Oh, I'm full of knowledge, Brooke. But I'm not givin' up my secrets that easily."

We continued like that as we ate. It was easy – natural. Brooke shared a story from her job in the city, something about a particularly difficult client and Peter Mantle, the managing partner, screwing things up that had us all laughing, and Cody kept the energy high with his excitement over the fishing trip. Caroline offered quiet observations here and there, and every now and then, she and Daisy would exchange a knowing look, both of them clearly enjoying how well everything was coming together.

After lunch, we all headed out to the porch, carrying our coffee and water glasses with us. The sun was starting to dip lower in the sky, casting a warm, golden light over everything. Cody, full from the meal, immediately darted off to play with Tink, tossing a ball for her to chase across the yard. The sound of his laughter filled the air as the dog barked excitedly, running circles around him.

I leaned back in one of the porch chairs, my

coffee mug warm in my hands, and looked out at the scene in front of me. Brooke, Daisy, and Caroline sat together on the porch swing, their conversation light and easy. They were laughing about something — probably some joke Daisy had made — and seeing them all like that, so at ease with each other, made me feel like I was exactly where I was supposed to be.

"You look happy," Brooke said softly, catching my eye from across the porch.

"I am," I replied, feeling the truth of it settle deep in my chest. "Everything feels… right."

Daisy, overhearing, nudged Caroline with her elbow. "He's probably just glad we're not makin' fun of his fishing skills anymore."

"I'm about to send you back into the kitchen, woman," I joked, and she laughed and stuck out her tongue at me.

The playful teasing continued, and I just sat back, enjoying the sound of it all. Cody's laughter, the girls' banter, the soft rustling of the trees in the breeze — it was the kind of peace I hadn't realized I'd been missing for so long. This was what I wanted. A home filled with love, with laughter, with the people I cared about most.

Brooke and Cody would be heading home again in a few hours, and I wasn't particularly looking forward to that. Daisy must have seen it, because she headed over to me and smiled.

"Say," she hummed, "I got an idea. Why don't you and Brooke leave Cody with us for a bit, hm? The two of you can head out and, well y'know, go on a little date or somethin'? Wouldn't that be nice?"

It was extremely sweet of her, and it was a perfect idea. It would allow us to reconnect a little, maybe talk through some things before she and Cody would head back to Louisville.

"That's a great idea, Daisy," I said, smiling at her. "And it's really sweet of you to suggest that."

"Well, I know how much she means to you, baby. I want you two to get along, and I'm willing to put in some work." She chuckled. "Although hangin' out with Caroline and Cody can hardly be called work, in my humble opinion."

I laughed and shot her a wink. "You're the best."

"Go on now, sugar lips," she hummed. "Cody

will be fine."

I stepped down from the porch and made my way over to Brooke, who was standing at the edge of the yard watching Cody toss the ball for Tink. She had a small smile on her face, her shoulders relaxed. She was having a good time; I knew her well enough to be able to tell. It felt like the perfect time.

"Hey," I said as I walked up next to her.

Brooke turned toward me, the sunlight catching her eyes. "Hey," she replied. "What's up?"

I smiled and nodded toward the house. "I was thinking… how about you and I head into town? Grab some dinner at Earl's? Just the two of us."

Brooke raised an eyebrow, clearly surprised. "Dinner? Just us?"

"Yeah," I said. "Daisy and Caroline offered to watch Cody for a bit. Figured we could use some time… you know, alone. Talk."

She hesitated for a moment, her gaze drifting back to Cody, who was laughing as Tink chased after the ball. "Are you sure? I mean, I don't want to impose on them."

I chuckled. "You're not imposing. Trust me, they're more than happy to spend time with Cody. Plus, you could use a break from all the 'Mom duty,' right?"

Brooke let out a small laugh and shook her head. "You know me too well." She glanced back at Cody, who was now trying to wrestle the ball away from Tink. "Alright, dinner sounds nice. Earl's, huh?"

"Just a good old small-town diner," I said with a grin. "A good meal, just the two of us, and no distractions."

Brooke smiled. "Okay, I'm in."

"Great," I said. "Let's go tell the others, and then we'll head out."

We made our way back toward the porch, where Daisy and Caroline were sitting, drinks in hand as they chatted. As Brooke and I approached, Daisy looked up with a playful grin.

"Y'all plannin' on sneakin' off without sayin' goodbye?" Daisy teased, her eyes sparkling with mischief.

I laughed. "We're just heading into town for dinner. You okay keeping an eye on Cody for a bit?"

"For sure!" Daisy replied with a wave of her hand. "We've got him covered. You two go on and enjoy yourselves."

Caroline nodded in agreement. "We'll keep him entertained. Don't worry."

Cody, hearing his name, came running over, Tink right behind him. "Where are you going, Dad?"

I crouched down, ruffling his hair. "Mom and I are going to have dinner in town. You'll be staying here with Daisy and Caroline. That sound good?"

Cody's face lit up. "Can we play in the field with Tink?"

Daisy chuckled. "I reckon we can manage that," she said, giving Cody a wink. "In fact, I think Tink couldn't be happier."

Cody grinned, clearly excited. "Okay! Have fun, Dad!" He turned to Brooke. "Bye, Mom!"

Brooke bent down and gave him a quick kiss on the head. "You be good, okay? Listen to Daisy and Caroline."

"I will!" Cody said, already bouncing on his toes with energy.

I stood up, giving the girls a grateful smile. "Thanks for this. We won't be gone too long."

"Take your time," Daisy said with a grin. "We'll keep things under control."

Caroline smiled softly. "Enjoy your dinner."

With that, Brooke and I turned and headed toward my red truck. As we reached it, I glanced at her and grinned. "Ready for some good ol' small-town dining?"

Brooke laughed as she climbed into the truck. "I think I can handle it."

"Good," I said, starting the engine. "Earl's isn't overwhelmingly gastronomic, but when it's simple you want, he knows how to make it."

Brooke laughed and nodded, looking thoughtful for a moment as she settled into the seat. "It'll be nice, I think… to just have a quiet meal. No rushing, no distractions."

"Exactly," I agreed as I pulled out of the driveway. "Just you, me, and some good food."

Brooke smiled, and we drove off, leaving behind the sounds of Cody's laughter as he played with Tink and the girls.

Chapter 22

The road stretched out before us, winding through the trees as the truck hummed along. The sun was starting to dip lower in the sky, and my stomach rumbled. I was in the mood for a good meal with some good company. Brooke sat beside me, her window cracked open slightly, letting the cool breeze in. The silence between us was comfortable, but I could tell she had something on her mind.

"So," I said, glancing over at her, "how's work been treating you lately?"

Brooke sighed, leaning her head back against the seat. "It's… exhausting, honestly. The clients, the cases, the constant deadlines…"

I nodded, keeping my eyes on the road. "You've been in it for a while now. You ever think about slowing down? Maybe cutting back a little?"

She let out a dry laugh. "I've thought about it. But I've worked so hard to get where I am, and part of me feels like if I slow down now, I'll be giving up on something. You know? Like all those years of climbing the corporate ladder would just be wasted."

"I get that," I said. "But what's the point of climbing if you're miserable at the top?"

Brooke was quiet for a moment, her fingers idly playing with the hem of her blouse. "Yeah… that's the question, isn't it? I don't know, Sean. Sometimes I feel like I'm stuck in this loop. Like I'm chasing something, but I don't even know what it is anymore."

I glanced over at her, catching the tiredness in

her eyes. "You don't have to chase it forever, Brooke. You could always make a change. There's nothing wrong with stepping back and reevaluating."

She sighed again, her expression softening. "I know you're right. It's just hard to let go of something that's been such a big part of my life for so long. But being out here, away from it all… it makes me realize how much I miss the quiet. The peace."

"That's what this place does," I said with a small smile. "Gives you the space to breathe, to figure out what really matters."

Brooke nodded slowly, her eyes drifting out the window. "Yeah, maybe that's what I need… some space to figure it all out."

I didn't push her further. I could tell she was wrestling with a lot, and this drive wasn't the time to solve everything. But it felt good knowing she was open to the idea of change. I wanted her to find peace, to be happy — not just for herself, but for Cody too.

We drove on in comfortable silence for a little longer, the town of Waycross just starting to come into view.

We pulled into the parking lot of Earl's, the place looking as familiar as ever with its broad front porch lined with rocking chairs. Brooke glanced around, taking it all in, and I could see the curiosity in her eyes. She'd never been here before, of course, so it was all new to her.

"This is Earl's?" she asked, eyebrows raised as she looked at the rustic exterior. "It's… charming."

I laughed. "That's one way to put it. It's an all-in-one kind of place – general store, bar, and diner. Earl's been running it forever."

She smiled softly. "Seems like the kind of place you'd love."

I parked the truck, and we got out, heading toward the entrance. The hand-painted sign above the door had that welcoming feel. As we walked inside, the cozy, cluttered space unfolded in front of us. Shelves stocked with goods lined one side of the store, and at the back, I could see the familiar dimly lit bar with a few locals sitting on stools, chatting quietly over drinks.

Earl himself was behind the counter, his bald

head gleaming under the low light, and his gray beard even wilder than normal. As soon as he spotted us, his face split into a wide grin.

"Well, look who it is!" he called out, waving us over. "Sean, my friend! Good to see you! And who's this lovely lady you've brought with you?"

I walked up to the counter, shaking his hand. "Good to see you too, Earl. This is Brooke. She's… well, she's visiting."

Brooke smiled and extended her hand. "Nice to meet you, Earl."

Earl gave her hand a firm shake, his grin never fading. "Pleasure's all mine, Brooke. Welcome to my humble little establishment. What can I get for you two tonight?"

"We're here for your famous burgers," I said, leaning against the counter.

Earl chuckled, rubbing his beard. "Ah, you know me too well. You want the usual, Sean? Double bacon cheeseburger?"

I nodded. "Yep, and Brooke will have the same."

Brooke shot me a playful look. "Oh, I guess I'm having the same, then."

I grinned at her. "Trust me, you'll love it."

Earl winked at Brooke. "You're in for a treat. I'll get those started for ya." He turned toward the kitchen, calling over his shoulder. "Go grab a seat in the back, and I'll bring 'em out when they're ready."

We headed to one of the small tables toward the back, settling into the wooden chairs as the low murmur of conversation filled the room. Brooke glanced around again, clearly still soaking in the atmosphere.

"This place is great," she said with a smile. "It feels… real. No pretense."

"That's why I like it," I replied. "It's simple, just like Waycross. No fuss, no frills."

She nodded, her eyes meeting mine. "I get it. I think I needed something like this."

As we got comfortable, Brooke leaned back in her chair, a small, nostalgic smile playing on her lips. "Remember that trip we took to France? Right before Cody was born?"

I chuckled. "Of course, I remember. That was a hell of a vacation."

Her eyes lit up with the memory. "I've been

thinking about it a lot lately. You know, walking through those little French towns, eating at those tiny cafés. It feels like a lifetime ago."

"It does," I agreed, leaning back in my chair as well. "I still think about those croissants we had in that village outside of Nice. They were unreal."

Brooke laughed. "And you wanted to buy the entire bakery. You ate three croissants in one sitting, if I remember correctly."

"I regret nothing," I said, grinning. "That was the best breakfast I've ever had. Though I think Earl's burgers might give those croissants a run for their money."

Brooke shook her head, still smiling. "That trip was the last time we really got to be carefree, wasn't it? Before the job, before the responsibilities piled on."

"Yeah," I said softly. "It was."

She paused, her smile fading slightly as her eyes grew more thoughtful. "I miss those days sometimes. When everything felt so open, so... full of possibility."

I reached across the table, taking her hand. "We can find that again, Brooke. Maybe not in the same way, but we can find our own kind of freedom here. Doesn't have to be France."

She gave my hand a gentle squeeze, her smile returning. "Maybe you're right."

Before we could say more, Earl came out of the kitchen, two steaming plates in hand. "Burgers are up!" he called, placing them on the table with a flourish. "Enjoy, you two."

We both thanked him, and as soon as the smell hit my nose, I knew we were in for a good meal. I glanced over at Brooke, and she raised her eyebrows, clearly impressed.

"You weren't kidding," she said, picking up her burger. "This might actually rival those croissants."

I laughed, taking a bite. "Told you. Earl knows what he's doing."

As we dug into our burgers, the conversation picked up again, the comfortable rhythm of familiarity between us.

Brooke took a bite, her eyes widening. "Okay, I take it back. This is way better than those croissants," she said, her voice muffled by a mouthful of food.

I laughed, wiping some sauce from the corner of my mouth. "Told you Earl's burgers were legendary. No one I know does it better."

She nodded, chewing thoughtfully for a moment before setting the burger down and wiping her hands. "You know, it's nice to sit like this. I feel like we haven't had a meal together in ages."

"Yeah." I leaned back, looking at her across the table. "Life got in the way."

Brooke gave a small, wistful smile. "It always does, doesn't it? I never thought things would get so… complicated. I always thought we'd have it figured out by now."

I nodded, understanding what she meant. "Yeah. Things don't always go as planned. But honestly? I think we did okay. And we have Cody to show for it. He's a gem."

Her expression softened as she glanced down at her plate. "Cody. He really changed everything, didn't he?"

"He did," I said, smiling. "For the better, though. I mean, yeah, it was a big adjustment. But I can't imagine life without him now."

Brooke looked up, her eyes warm. "Same here. It's like… the moment he was born, all the stuff we thought mattered just faded away. It became about him. About making sure he was happy and taken care of."

"Yeah. I remember the first night we brought him home," I said, chuckling at the memory. "Neither of us knew what we were doing. We were up every hour because we thought every little sound he made meant something was wrong."

Brooke laughed softly. "God, I was so paranoid back then. I was convinced he wasn't getting enough sleep or eating enough, and you kept trying to calm me down."

"Yeah, I kept saying he was fine, but I was just as worried," I admitted with a grin. "I'd be lying if I said I didn't spend more than a few nights checking on him while you were sleeping."

She smiled at that, her eyes softening. "You were always such a good dad, Sean. Even when things got tough between us… you never let any of it affect how you were with Cody. I always admired that."

I shrugged, taking another bite of my burger. "He's my kid. I'd move mountains for him."

Brooke nodded, her gaze drifting for a moment as if lost in thought. "I think about how different things could've been, you know? If we hadn't had him… I don't think we'd still be connected like we are."

"Maybe not," I said. "I think we would though. What we have goes deep, Brooke. But I'll admit he brought out the best in both of us. Even when things weren't great, we always found common ground when it came to him."

She smiled, a little wistful. "He's the best thing we ever did."

"No argument there," I said softly.

We both sat in comfortable silence for a moment, finishing our burgers, letting the weight of the conversation settle between us. There was a sense of peace in talking about Cody, reflecting on what he'd given us — even if everything else hadn't turned out the way we planned.

Brooke looked up, catching my eye again. "I'm really glad you've been such a big part of his life, Sean. He needs you."

"I need him, too," I replied. "He's what keeps me grounded."

She smiled at that, nodding. "Yeah. He does that for me too."

After we finished our burgers, Earl came around with a fresh pot of coffee. We both accepted, and as we sipped, the conversation drifted naturally.

"You know," Brooke started, stirring a bit of sugar into her mug, "I was watching Daisy and Caroline with Cody earlier. They're really good with him, Sean. I mean, like, *really* good."

I nodded, setting my cup down. "Yeah, they are. Daisy's got this easy way with kids, doesn't she? Always full of energy, always making things fun. She's like his personal cheerleader."

Brooke laughed softly. "I noticed that. She's so bubbly, it's contagious. And she's gonna teach Cody how to *farm,* which is just the sweetest. I mean, he's over the moon just thinking about it."

I chuckled. "Yeah, she's been on him about getting his hands dirty, showing him the ropes. She's great at turning everything into an adventure for him."

Brooke nodded, taking a sip of her coffee. "And

Caroline… she's more reserved, but there's something really calming about her. Cody seems to trust her. He was telling her about his books earlier, and she was hanging on every word like it was the most interesting thing in the world."

I smiled. "That's Caroline for you. She might be quiet, but she's got a way of making people feel heard. She's patient, and she gets Cody's quieter side. He can talk to her about things he might not always bring up with Daisy."

Brooke tilted her head, a thoughtful look crossing her face. "They balance each other out. Daisy with all her energy, and Caroline with that calm, steady vibe."

"Exactly," I said. "It's one of the things that works so well between them. And with Cody, they just know how to bring out the best in him."

Brooke smiled softly. "It's nice to see him so happy with them. I was a little worried, at first, about how he'd adjust… you know, to you having these relationships, but he seems to be thriving."

"Yeah, I was concerned too," I admitted. "But he's handled it better than I expected. I think part of it is because Daisy and Caroline don't try to replace anything. They've just slotted into his life in a way that feels natural."

Brooke nodded, her fingers tracing the rim of her coffee cup. "I can see that. And, honestly… it's a relief. I feel better knowing that when he's here with you, he's got all this support. That there's more than just you looking out for him."

I smiled, feeling a warmth in my chest. "They really care about him, Brooke. That's for sure."

She met my gaze, her expression soft. "Yeah. I can see that. It makes me feel… good."

I leaned back in my chair, watching Brooke as she sipped her coffee, the warm light from the diner making her seem all the more beautiful. An idea sparked, something fired on by nostalgia, and I glanced over at the old jukebox in the corner. It hadn't been used the entire time we'd been here, but I knew Earl kept it stocked with classics.

"I've got an idea," I said, pushing back from the table.

Brooke raised an eyebrow, curious. "What are you up to?"

"You'll see."

I walked over to the jukebox, scanning the selection until I found what I was looking for — an old country song we used to listen to all the time. It wasn't flashy or overly romantic; in fact, it held a hint of sweet sadness like only this kind of music can.

It was us. The kind of song that brought back memories of long drives and quiet nights. I dropped a few quarters in, and the familiar tune started playing, filling the small space with its soft twang.

Brooke's eyes lit up as soon as she recognized the song. "You remember this one?"

"How could I not?" I said, holding out a hand. "Care to dance?"

She hesitated for just a second, but then a smile tugged at the corner of her lips. "I'd love to."

She placed her hand in mine, and I led her to the empty space near the jukebox, away from the tables. It wasn't exactly a dance floor, but it didn't matter. The moment I pulled her close, everything else faded away.

We swayed slowly, caught up in the rhythm of the song. Her head rested lightly against my chest, and I wrapped an arm around her waist, holding her close. For a few minutes, it was just the two of us — no past, no future, just the present. The quiet intimacy of the moment made the room feel smaller, like we were in our own world, surrounded by the soft notes coming from the jukebox and the gentle clink of dishes in the background.

"This takes me back," Brooke murmured, her breath warm against my neck.

I nodded, my chin brushing the top of her head. "Me too. Feels like old times."

We moved slowly, neither of us in any rush for the moment to end. The song played on, and I could feel her relaxing more with each step, her body fitting naturally against mine, just like it always had. The way she felt in my arms, it was like we hadn't missed a beat.

As the last notes of the song drifted away, I pulled back slightly to look at her. Her eyes met mine, soft and full of something unspoken. Without thinking, I leaned down, closing the space between us, and kissed her again. It wasn't rushed or filled with the weight of everything unsaid — it was just… right.

Familiar, but new at the same time.

When we finally pulled apart, she smiled, her forehead resting against mine for a brief moment before stepping back.

"Sean," she whispered, her voice barely audible over the fading music.

I didn't need her to say anything else. We both knew what that dance had meant, what that kiss had stirred.

As we drove back toward the house, the soft hum of the truck's engine was soothing to us both. Brooke stared out the window, her fingers drumming lightly on her knee. The moonlight outside made the landscape pass in soft shadows, but inside the cab, things felt quieter. More real.

She sighed, breaking the silence. "One night just doesn't feel like enough."

I glanced over at her, keeping my hands steady on the wheel. "Yeah, I get that. It's been nice having you and Cody here. Feels like… well, it feels like it used to."

She turned her head to look at me, her

expression a mix of wistfulness and frustration. "I didn't expect it to feel this way. I thought it would be good, but I didn't realize how much I'd miss it once we had to leave. I don't want it to end so soon."

I nodded, understanding what she was saying. "It's tough. Having you two here, just living for a bit like this… It's been good. But we can do this again. Doesn't have to be the last time."

Brooke let out a small laugh, shaking her head. "I know, I know. I just feel like I'm only just starting to figure it all out, and now I'm going back to Louisville. It's hard to switch gears like that."

"Yeah," I said quietly, gripping the steering wheel a little tighter. "But we don't have to rush anything, Brooke. I want you two to come back when you're ready. We'll plan something soon. It doesn't have to be just one night."

She leaned her head back against the seat, staring up at the ceiling for a second. "I'm just… I don't know. I'm torn, I guess. I love my job, but this — what we've had today — this is what I've been missing. Seeing Cody so happy, and just… us being together."

I glanced at her again. "That's what matters most, isn't it? You, Cody, and us finding time for this, making it work. We'll make more time. Just because you have to leave now doesn't mean it's the end of anything."

She sighed softly and looked over at me, her voice quieter now. "I know. I guess I'm just afraid that once I go back to the city, life's going to take over again. You know how it is."

"I do," I agreed. "But we'll make it work, Brooke. We've got time. We'll make sure Cody spends more time here, that *you* spend more time here. If you want that."

She smiled, her eyes softening. "I do want that, Sean. More than I thought I would."

I squeezed her hand briefly, trying to reassure her. "Then we'll figure it out. No pressure. We'll take it slow. I'm not going anywhere."

She chuckled lightly, but there was something tender in her voice. "Thanks for saying that. I know you mean it. It's just hard to juggle everything sometimes. I don't want to miss out on this, on Cody being so happy here… on what we could have."

I kept my eyes on the road but gave her hand another squeeze. "You won't miss out. Cody loves it here, and he loves being with you. And we'll work out more time for you to be here too. We're just getting started."

She looked down at our hands, her thumb brushing over my knuckles for a moment. "It's funny, isn't it? I spent all this time building a life in the city, thinking that's what I needed. But today… today felt different. I felt more at home here than I have in a long time."

I nodded. "This place has a way of doing that. And you're always welcome here. Both of you. That's never going to change."

She smiled softly. "I know. It's just hard to switch back and forth."

"We don't have to figure it all out tonight," I said. "We'll take our time. We'll plan another visit soon."

She sighed again, this time with a bit more relief. "I'd like that. More time… more of this."

I grinned. "More of us."

She laughed lightly. "Yeah… more of us."

Chapter 23

As night closed in, the time to say goodbye had come. Brooke and Cody stood on the porch, ready to head back to the city. Tink circled around Cody excitedly, as if sensing he was about to leave and wanting to soak up every last minute with her playmate.

Daisy leaned against the porch railing, her arms

crossed, a soft smile playing on her lips as she watched them. Caroline stood beside her, looking a little more reserved but equally warm. We'd all spent the day together, and while it felt like the right time to say goodbye, there was a weight of reluctance in the air.

Cody, still full of energy, gave Tink one last pat before bounding up the steps to me. "Bye, Dad! Can I come back next weekend?" he asked, practically bouncing on his toes.

I chuckled, ruffling his hair. "Of course, buddy. Anytime you want, you're welcome here," I said. Then I turned to Brooke, giving her a soft look. "Just let me know, and we'll make it happen."

Brooke caught my eyes, her expression warmer than it had been all day. "We really enjoyed this, Sean. It was..." She hesitated for a second, as if searching for the right words. "It was nice, being here. Peaceful. I think it's just what Cody and I needed."

I could see the sincerity in her eyes, and it filled me with a sense of hope. I smiled, nodding. "I'm glad you both had a good time. You're always welcome here, Brooke. Both of you. Whenever you feel like coming out, just say the word."

She nodded, her lips curling into a soft smile. "Thanks, Sean. I know that. I just… I need to figure things out, you know? It's a lot to process."

"Take your time," I said, my voice steady, calm. "There's no rush. Just know this place is here, whenever you want it."

She gave a small laugh, but there was something deeper in her eyes — something I knew she wasn't quite ready to talk about. "You've always been patient with me," she said softly, almost more to herself than to me. Then she looked up, her blue eyes meeting mine. "I appreciate that. I really do."

Daisy, ever the lighthearted one, chimed in with a grin. "Hey, Cody, you gonna come back and help me out on the farm next time? You promised, remember?"

Cody's face lit up. "Yeah! I'm gonna milk the cows, right?"

Daisy laughed. "You bet, little man. We'll have you wranglin' heifers in no time. And I'll teach you how to feed the chickens too. You'll be a real farmhand."

Cody's excitement was contagious, and I could

see the spark in his eyes. "I can't wait! It's gonna be so much fun!" He turned to Brooke, tugging on her sleeve. "Mom, can we come back soon? Please?"

Brooke smiled down at him, brushing a hand over his hair. "We'll see, Cody. We'll see. I think it's safe to say we'll be back before too long, though."

"Promise?" he pressed, his voice hopeful.

She laughed softly, nodding. "Promise."

Caroline, quiet but thoughtful as ever, stepped forward, her voice gentle. "Cody, next time you're here, I'll show you some of my favorite books. I've got a whole collection that you might like. Maybe we can spend some time reading together."

Cody's eyes lit up again. "Really? I love reading! What kind of books do you have?"

Caroline smiled, looking a little more at ease. "Oh, lots of different ones. Adventure stories, mysteries… I think you'd like them."

Brooke gave Caroline a grateful look, her voice soft as she said, "That sounds like a great idea. Thank you, Caroline."

Caroline blushed slightly but nodded. "It's

nothing. I'm looking forward to it."

Cody, clearly eager, darted over to give Daisy and Caroline quick hugs. "Bye, Daisy! Bye, Caroline! I'll see you both soon!"

Daisy hugged him back, ruffling his hair. "You take care now, champ. Don't forget about those cows."

Caroline gave him a shy smile, patting his shoulder. "See you soon, Cody."

As Cody ran back to the black sedan, Brooke lingered for a moment longer, her eyes still on me. I could feel something unspoken between us, a kind of quiet understanding that didn't need to be put into words.

I took a step closer, my voice dropping just a little. "You okay?"

She nodded, her gaze meeting mine. "Yeah. I'm just… I'm glad we did this, Sean. I wasn't sure how it would feel, coming out here, but it was good. It felt right."

I smiled, feeling that warmth in my chest again. "I'm glad to hear that. It was good having you here. I missed you."

Brooke looked down for a second, then back up

at me, and before I could say anything else, she leaned in. I had meant to kiss her cheek, something light, casual — but she turned her head slightly, and our lips brushed, soft but full of meaning. For a moment, time seemed to slow down.

When we pulled away, I could see a slight blush coloring her cheeks, and I knew she was thinking about last night. I could tell. She hadn't said anything about watching me with Daisy and Caroline, and I wasn't going to bring it up — didn't want to embarrass her. But I knew. And I had a feeling *she knew* that I knew.

"Take care, Brooke," I said quietly.

She nodded, her eyes holding mine for a moment longer before she turned to head toward the car. "You too, Sean. We'll talk soon."

As she climbed into the driver's seat and started the engine, Cody waved one last time from the backseat. "Bye, Dad!"

I waved back, smiling. "See you soon, buddy."

As the car disappeared down the driveway, I stood there with Daisy and Caroline by my side, feeling the echoes of the day lingering in the air.

And I was full of hope for the future.

Chapter 24

The shrill sound of the alarm by the front door pierced the silence of the night, jolting me awake. Instinct kicked in immediately, and I was out of bed in an instant. Beside me, Daisy stirred, her hand reaching for me in the dark.

"Sean?" she murmured, her voice thick with sleep but already laced with concern. "What is it?"

"Stay here," I said firmly, already moving toward the closet where I kept the Mossberg. "Both of you. Stay put."

Caroline sat up on the other side of the bed, her eyes wide but alert. "What's happening?" she whispered.

"I'll check it out. Lock the bedroom door behind me. Don't come out until I tell you it's clear," I said, checking the shotgun's chamber with practiced ease.

Daisy nodded, her expression shifting to one of steely resolve, but I could see the worry in her eyes. Caroline, always more cautious, was already moving to lock the door as I made my way out of the room, shotgun in hand.

The house was still dark, only the faint glow of the moon seeping through the windows. My steps were quick but measured as I moved down the stairs, my senses heightened. The alarm was still blaring, echoing through the house. My gut told me this wasn't a false alarm, and I felt the weight of my instincts guiding me forward.

As I approached the living room, I caught movement out of the corner of my eye. My pulse quickened. I slowed my steps, raising the Mossberg to my shoulder as I turned into the living room.

There, crouched by the doorway, was a goblin — its grotesque form hunched low as it fumbled with something in its gnarled hands.

For a split second, the creature looked up, its yellow eyes locking onto mine, and it hissed, baring jagged teeth.

I didn't give it the chance to react. My finger squeezed the trigger, and the Mossberg roared, the shotgun blast ripping through the goblin's chest. The creature let out a guttural screech as it crumpled to the ground, twitching for a moment before going still. Blood pooled around its small, twisted body.

And there was that infernal ringing in my ears again.

I stood there, shotgun still raised, waiting for any other signs of more intruders. But the house was still now. Slowly, my hearing recovered as the goblin corpse faded away, leaving only blood. The creature had been fumbling with my alarm system, stupidly trying to dismantle it, even though it had already gone off.

Keeping my guard up, I moved swiftly to check the rest of the house. I cleared each room with precision, keeping close to the walls, buttonhooking through doorways, and making sure I had a firm grip on my weapon in case something would dart out from the shadows and attempt to disarm me or take control of the firearm. The kitchen, the living room, the front porch – everything was empty.

Once I was sure the house was secure, I stepped outside, the cool night air hitting my face as I scanned the property. I moved through the yard, checking every corner, every shadow for any sign of movement. The woods loomed in the distance, dark and foreboding, but nothing stirred.

Satisfied there were no other immediate threats, I made my way back inside, locking the door behind me and heading back upstairs.

As I reached the bedroom, the door cracked open, and Daisy's face appeared in the dim light. "Sean?" she asked, her voice tense.

"It's clear," I said, stepping into the room and closing the door behind me. "One goblin. Took care of it."

Caroline let out a shaky breath, her hand still on the doorknob. "Are you sure there aren't more?"

I nodded, placing the Mossberg against the wall. "I cleared the house. Nothing else inside. But we need to stay on high alert. I'll be heading to Harper's first thing in the morning to track those goblins down. This is getting too close for comfort, and now we finally have a set of tracks to follow."

Daisy crossed the room, her arms wrapping around me in a tight embrace. "I'm glad you're okay," she murmured against my chest.

I kissed the top of her head, my mind already racing through the next steps. "We'll handle it," I said, my voice firm. "Tomorrow, I'm going to get Harper. We'll track them down and put an end to this."

The sun was barely up when I pulled my truck onto the dirt road leading to Harper's place. The events of last night weighed heavily on me – too heavily to wait another day. We needed to get moving while the trail was fresh.

When I reached Harper's cottage, the old place

looked as it always did — like something out of time. Smoke drifted lazily from the chimney, curling into the crisp morning air. I parked and climbed out, the gravel crunching under my boots as I made my way to the door. I gave it a firm knock, knowing Harper would be up by now.

The door creaked open a moment later, and there stood Harper, his long gray hair tied back in its usual ponytail, a look of curiosity and mild concern on his face. "Sean," he greeted, glancing me up and down. "Bit early, ain't it?"

"Not for this," I replied, stepping inside when he motioned me through. "We've got a problem. Had a goblin at my place last night — triggered the alarm by the front door. I took care of it, but it got way too close."

Harper's face darkened. "Damn," he muttered, shutting the door behind us. "You sure it was alone?"

I shook my head. "Not sure. I killed it fast and checked the perimeter, but there might have been more in the forest. That's why I came here first thing. We need to track them, Harper — today. I'm not waiting around for another attack."

Harper rubbed his chin, eyes narrowing in thought. “Figures they’d get bolder,” he muttered, half to himself. “If one of ‘em was bold enough to hit your house, they probably came in a group.” He turned and walked toward the old wooden cabinet on the far wall. “We need to track them down.”

I followed him across the room, watching as he opened the cabinet to reveal an M1 Garand rifle nestled inside. Harper pulled it out carefully, checking the action and giving it a quick look over. “Tracks should be good to follow,” he continued, pulling out a box of ammunition. “Goblins are stealthy creatures, but they leave signs — broken branches, disturbed earth, scat. We’ll find something.”

“I was hoping you’d say that,” I said, feeling a little bit of tension ease in my chest. If anyone could find those goblins, it was Harper.

He nodded, slipping a couple of extra clips holding cartridges for his rifle into his jacket pocket and then grabbing a leather satchel from the table. “Daisy and Caroline coming with us?”

“They’re ready back at my place,” I confirmed.

"Both armed and eager. Figured the more of us, the better."

"Good call," Harper said, slinging the Garand over his shoulder. "You've got some sharp girls on your side. Extra eyes'll help in case the trail's harder to pick up."

As Harper secured the satchel across his chest, I glanced around his small cottage, the walls lined with hunting trophies and old, weathered maps of the forest surrounding Waycross. He'd been living here for years, but it felt like this place had been the hub of his life's work — tracking, guiding, knowing the woods better than most men knew their own houses.

"Got everything?" I asked as he grabbed a knife from the shelf and strapped it to his belt.

He gave me a quick nod. "All set. Let's not waste any daylight."

We stepped outside, and the crisp morning air hit me, along with the distant smell of damp earth and pine. Harper shut the door behind him, and we walked to my truck.

"Think they'll come back?" Harper asked as I started the engine.

"They were bold enough to come once," I said, keeping my eyes on the road ahead. "I'd be a fool to think they won't try again. That's why we need to get ahead of them."

Harper grunted, leaning back in his seat as the truck bumped along the dirt road. "Goblins are smart in their own way. But they're also cowardly. We take the fight to 'em, make it clear they're not welcome, they might just scatter. Or," he added with a grim smile, "we could wipe 'em out entirely."

"That's the plan," I said, my voice hard. "I'm not stopping until we've cleared the area."

The drive back to my place was mostly quiet after that, though every now and then Harper would mutter something about the weather or the state of the forest, as if mentally cataloging every detail for when we hit the trail. I could tell he was already thinking about the hunt, about how we'd track them, what we'd find. His experience as a tracker was obvious, and I was glad we had him with us.

As we pulled into the driveway, I could see Daisy and Caroline already outside, standing near the front porch. Daisy had her shotgun slung over her shoulder, and Caroline stood by her side. They were alert, ready, and the look of determination on their faces mirrored my own.

Harper climbed out of the truck, his sharp eyes scanning the yard as he nodded in approval at the girls' preparedness. "Morning, ladies," he said, giving them a quick once-over. "You two ready for a hunt?"

"More than ready," Daisy replied, her lips curving into a small, fierce smile. "Let's track these little bastards down."

"We are," Caroline added softly but firmly.

Harper adjusted the strap of his rifle, glancing toward the woods that bordered my property. "We'll find the trail," he said.

I nodded, my gaze shifting between the three of them. "Stay alert. The moment we find a sign, we follow it. This ends today."

Chapter 25

We set out into the forest, moving in a tight formation with Harper leading the way. His M1 Garand rested comfortably in his hands as he scanned the ground, his eyes flicking from the path ahead to the trees surrounding us, then back to the forest floor. The man had a sixth sense for the woods. Every time we stepped deeper into the forest, I felt the tension between us, but Harper moved like he belonged here, completely in his element.

Hopefully, more time here would make me just as comfortable here as he was.

Daisy walked just behind me, her shotgun gripped tightly in her hands, eyes wide and alert. Caroline, unarmed but no less focused, stayed close to Daisy, her sharp gaze moving between the treetops and the ground. I could feel the intensity radiating off her as she focused on any movement or sound that might signal danger. She wasn't armed, but that didn't make her any less valuable out here. She had a quick mind.

The thick underbrush rustled with our passage, and every now and then, Harper would crouch low, studying the signs on the forest floor. His movements were slow and deliberate, the old soldier in him coming to life as he expertly traced the goblin's path.

We'd been walking for nearly half an hour when Harper finally paused, kneeling beside a patch of disturbed earth. He gestured for us to stop, raising his hand without saying a word. The forest was eerily quiet, save for the occasional rustling of leaves in the wind.

"What is it?" I asked in a low voice, keeping my Mossberg at the ready.

Harper squinted at the ground, running his fingers through the dirt. "Goblin tracks," he murmured. "Recent. Looks like the one that hit your place didn't come alone."

Daisy leaned over my shoulder, her voice just as low. "How many, you think?"

Harper didn't answer immediately. He studied the tracks for another moment before finally standing up. "At least three, maybe four. They're moving in a small group. Scouts, most likely. Could be more of 'em further in."

My jaw tightened. "So, they're watching the area."

"Looks that way," Harper replied, his voice grim.

I scanned the trees around us. Every sound seemed amplified now, every shadow a potential threat. I could feel the weight of my Mossberg in my hands. "We keep moving?"

Harper nodded. "We follow the tracks. They're

heading deeper into the woods — probably back to wherever they're holed up. If we're lucky, we can find their camp and put an end to this."

With that, we moved forward again, the tension growing as we ventured deeper into the forest. The trees thickened around us, their towering forms casting long shadows over the trail. Harper was a few paces ahead, his rifle at the ready, scanning the path for more signs. Every now and then, he'd stop to examine a broken branch or a patch of disturbed leaves, confirming we were still on the right track.

"We're getting close," he muttered after another few minutes of silent walking. "These tracks are fresh. Real fresh."

Daisy's shotgun clicked softly as she adjusted her grip. "You think they know we're following them?"

"Goblins aren't stupid," Harper replied. "They might not know exactly, but they've got a sense for danger. They'll be keeping an eye out."

Caroline spoke up quietly from the back. "What do we do if they try to ambush us?"

"They won't get the chance," I said firmly,

though I kept my voice low. "We're not here to play games. If we see them, we take them down before they can pull anything."

Harper nodded in agreement. "That's the way to do it. You meet your adversary with determined force, and you will win."

We pressed forward, the woods growing darker as the morning sun struggled to break through the thick canopy overhead. The silence around us was oppressive now; every sound, every movement put my senses on edge.

Harper paused again, crouching low and examining a set of fresh footprints. "They're close," he murmured, eyes narrowing. "Real close."

We pushed deeper into the woods, the underbrush becoming thicker with each step. Harper's sharp eyes flicked from one sign to the next — broken branches, scattered footprints, and the occasional discarded bone or scrap of cloth. The signs were clear now. The goblins had passed through recently, and in numbers.

Harper paused beside a tree, crouching to examine the ground. "Look at this," he said, pointing to a set of tracks. "Heavier movement here. More of 'em, too. They're clustering."

I knelt beside him, narrowing my eyes at the prints. "A larger group?"

"Definitely. And look over there." Harper pointed toward a small clearing ahead. "Remnants of a fire pit. They've camped here recently."

I stood, scanning the tree line. "We're getting close, aren't we?"

Harper nodded, standing as well. "Close enough that we need to be careful."

Daisy stepped forward, her grip tight on her shotgun as she glanced around the clearing. "How far, you think? They close by?"

"Not far," Harper replied. "Their main camp should be just ahead. Maybe half a mile, no more than that."

Caroline shifted, her voice calm but tense. "Should we keep moving together?"

I glanced at Harper. "We need to scout ahead. Can you two hold back here?"

Daisy nodded, her face set in determination. "We'll be fine. You two go. Just don't do anything stupid."

I smirked. "Never."

Caroline gave a small smile, though there was concern in her eyes. "Be careful."

Harper slung his rifle into a more ready position and gestured toward the thicker part of the woods. "Let's see what we're dealing with."

I nodded at the girls, then motioned for Harper to lead the way. Together, we crept forward, moving with practiced precision, the signs of goblin activity growing more frequent with each step.

Harper and I moved quietly through the thick underbrush, the woods closing in around us as we followed the faint signs. We heard some growling up ahead, and we exchanged a look that conveyed we both knew they were close.

Then, we saw them.

Ahead, crouched low and moving cautiously through the trees, was a group of six goblins. Their hunched forms darted in and out of shadows, noses sniffing the air, gnarled hands gripping crude weapons. They were scouting, their yellow eyes flicking around, on high alert but unaware we were watching.

I crouched beside Harper, my back pressed against a tree. He raised his hand, showing me the number — six. I nodded. It wasn't too many, but we had to handle this right.

"We head back," Harper whispered. His eyes stayed on the goblins, watching their movements. "Set up an ambush. They're comin' this way."

I nodded again, keeping my voice low. "We'll surprise them. Clean and quick."

We slipped back the way we came, moving fast and quiet. When we reached Daisy and Caroline, Harper gave a short signal, and they both tensed, ready for action.

"Six goblins up ahead," I said quietly. "Coming this way. We'll set up here and catch them off guard. I'll use the Wood Sigil to fabricate us some cover."

Daisy readied her shotgun, her grip firm. Caroline, while unarmed, gave a determined nod. She knew her role was to stay hidden, but her focus was sharp.

I knelt by the nearest tree stumps, placing my hand on one. The pulse of the Wood Sigil surged through me, and the energy from the earth responded. Slowly, I manipulated the wood, making the stumps grow taller, widening them into natural barriers for us to use as cover but keeping their appearance natural. The wood groaned softly as it shifted and took shape, offering perfect concealment. I would have preferred making a few traps, but this was all we had time for.

Daisy took position behind one stump, shotgun resting on her shoulder, her eyes narrowed with focus. Harper settled beside her, his M1 Garand ready. I moved to the opposite side, keeping my Mossberg steady, watching the path the goblins would take.

"Wait for my signal," Harper muttered, his eyes locked ahead.

We crouched there in silence, the woods eerily still, waiting for the moment. And then, the goblins came into view, creeping through the trees, unaware they were walking into a trap. I counted each one as they moved closer — six.

Harper raised his hand, holding it steady as the goblins moved into range.

Closer. Closer.

Now.

Harper's hand dropped, and in one smooth motion, I squeezed the trigger of the Mossberg. The blast ripped through the quiet of the woods, and the lead goblin's chest exploded in a mess of gore. It let out a guttural scream as it collapsed. Before the others could react, Harper fired, his Garand cracking sharply through the air as another goblin fell, the bullet punching clean through its skull.

Daisy wasted no time. Her shotgun kicked back as she fired, taking a third goblin straight through the neck, blood spraying out in an arc as it dropped.

The remaining three goblins panicked, screeching in confusion as they scrambled for cover, but there was no escape. Harper fired again, dropping one of them mid-sprint, its body hitting the ground with a heavy thud. The fifth goblin tried to dart into the shadows, but I was faster. I swung the Mossberg, aiming at its back, and pulled the trigger. The blast hit it square in the spine, sending it flying forward into a tree. It twitched for a moment, then went still.

The final goblin let out a terrified shriek and tried to flee into the forest. Daisy pivoted quickly, her shotgun firing off one last round. The shot tore through the goblin's shoulder, spinning it around before it collapsed onto the ground, gasping for breath. She took two steps forward and finished it off with a clean shot to the head.

Silence settled back over the woods, the only sound the distant rustling of leaves and the fading echo of gunfire. We stayed crouched for a moment longer, scanning the area for any signs of more. When none came, Harper stood, his rifle still at the ready.

"All down," he muttered, eyes sweeping the carnage.

I rose from behind the stump, keeping my Mossberg ready just in case. We moved carefully toward the bodies, checking each one to ensure they were truly dead. The goblins lay in grotesque, twisted piles, their crude weapons scattered around them. They were ugly little things, but they were dangerous in numbers — and these six wouldn't be the last.

I crouched beside one of the corpses, turning it over with my boot. The goblin's eyes were glazed over, blood pooling around its twisted form. "Anything useful?" I asked, already knowing the answer.

Daisy kicked at another body, her expression one of disgust. "Nothing. Just scraps."

Harper wiped his brow with the back of his hand, slinging his rifle over his shoulder. "Nothing worth keeping. They're traveling light."

I nodded, standing up and letting out a breath. "Means their main camp isn't far. Let's keep moving."

As the corpses faded, we moved on — in the direction they had come from.

Chapter 26

We crouched low against the rocky outcrop, the cool stone pressed against our backs as we looked down into the hidden valley. The goblin camp sprawled before us, larger and more organized than any of us had expected. It was a mess of crude tents, makeshift lean-tos, and fire pits scattered between rocky outcrops that shielded it from casual view. Goblins milled about between them, grunting to one another in their guttural language, clearly unbothered by any idea of a threat.

The whole area seemed alive with movement. A couple of goblins were tending a large fire in the center, spitting and roasting something that looked like a small deer. Others were sharpening and crafting crude weapons – rusted blades and jagged clubs – while a few lounged around, laughing and jostling each other with bony elbows. Near the mouth of the cave that dominated the far side of the valley, a larger goblin, clearly the leader, stood barking orders at a pair of smaller, scrawnier creatures.

"That's a damn lot of them," Daisy whispered, barely keeping her voice under control as she scanned the camp with narrowed eyes. "I count at least two dozen. Maybe more hiding in that cave."

I glanced over at her, my mind racing. She wasn't wrong. This was far bigger than we'd anticipated. And if they were all as bold as the scouts we'd just ambushed, then letting them continue unchecked wasn't an option.

"We expected a camp," I said, my voice low, "but this? It's a full-on settlement."

Harper crouched next to me, peering down through a set of old binoculars. "Yeah," he muttered, his voice grim. "Looks like they've been here a while. Too long, honestly. They're dug in pretty good."

Caroline, sitting back against the rock behind us, bit her lip as she took in the sight of the cave entrance, where goblins disappeared and reappeared regularly, dragging bundles of sticks, stones, and other supplies inside. "That cave..." she murmured. "There's probably more inside, isn't there? A lot more."

I shook my head. "A cave like that? It's only a small one. Doubt there's going to be many — maybe a few. Still, we've got to assume what we see here is just the surface."

Harper nodded in agreement.

Daisy gripped the shotgun tighter in her hands. "So, what's the plan? We can't just charge in there with the four of us. We'd be overwhelmed in seconds."

Harper lowered the binoculars, his eyes hard as

he surveyed the layout below. "We don't have the numbers to go in head-on. Even with the element of surprise, we'd get swarmed before we made it halfway through the camp. We need a strategy."

I stared down at the camp, my mind working through the options. Charging in wasn't an option – that much was clear. But leaving them to continue building strength wasn't either. I glanced at the cave mouth again, an idea forming in the back of my mind.

I beckoned everyone to follow, and we retreated from the ridge in silence, moving low and fast until the goblin camp was well behind us. Once we were a good distance away, I raised a hand, signaling for us to stop. We crouched around a fallen log, forming a rough circle. The air was tense, everyone waiting for the next move.

"Alright," Harper muttered, his eyes flicking between us. "We've got a problem. There's no way we're getting in there guns blazing. That camp's too big. We'd get overrun before we could even make a dent."

Daisy glanced back the way we'd come, adjusting her grip on the shotgun. "You think they'll notice that patrol's missing soon?" She sounded nervous, but her face was calm, focused. "If they start looking for them, we're in trouble."

Harper scratched his chin, eyes narrowing. "Could be minutes, could be hours. Depends how often they check in."

"We need a plan," I said, lowering my voice. "We can't just wait around for them to figure it out. But we also can't rush in there without something solid."

Daisy nodded, but she wasn't done with her question. "What if they send another patrol?" She turned toward me. "We need to do something now before they start sniffing around."

"That's why we need to act fast," I said. "The patrol we took out? They're not going to find the bodies — they disappeared. That buys us time. But it won't be long before someone notices they're missing."

"Then what do you have in mind?" Caroline asked, her voice steady but cautious. She was watching me closely, waiting to hear something concrete.

"I've got an idea," I said, glancing between

them. "We don't have the numbers to take them head-on, but we can even the odds with a little help from my magic."

Daisy tilted her head. "What are you thinking? Something like what you did with the stumps earlier?"

"Exactly," I replied. "I can manipulate the trees and roots around their camp, set up some traps. We create barriers, block their escape routes, maybe funnel them into one area where we can control the fight. If we do it right, we'll force them into a kill zone."

Harper raised an eyebrow. "How long you reckon that'll take? Goblins are sneaky. They'll catch on quick if they hear something, or if they send someone else out to scout."

"Not long," I said. "I can move the wood fast if we pick the right spots. We just need to decide where we want to lure them and how we can maximize our firepower."

Caroline looked thoughtful, her brow furrowed. "We need to make sure they can't scatter. If they split up and start hiding in the woods, we'll lose track of them."

I nodded. “Right. We need to contain them in one spot.”

Daisy spoke up again, more confident now. “So, we’re talking about setting up traps around the perimeter of the camp, right? Then what? We lure them out somehow?”

“Exactly,” I said. “We don’t go inside the camp. We stay on the outside, let the traps do the work. Once they start panicking, we hit them hard.”

Harper grunted in agreement. “If we set the traps right, we can pick them off before they even know what hit ’em. But like you said, we’ll need to be quick. No telling when that missing patrol’s gonna raise suspicion.”

Caroline chewed her lip. “And what if the patrol was due to check in? If they’re already late, they’ll send more goblins out to investigate.”

“That’s the risk we take,” I said, glancing at Harper. “But if we set everything up fast enough, we can use it to our advantage. When they send another patrol, they’ll walk right into the traps.”

Harper gave a small nod. “Sounds like a solid plan. But we’ll need to be damn careful. If we make too much noise setting those traps, they’ll come out before we're ready."

"Then we move quietly," I said, turning back to the group. "Harper and I will set up the traps. Daisy, you and Caroline keep watch. If you spot anything – or anyone – coming out of the camp, you signal us."

Daisy smirked. "I can handle that."

"Alright," I said, looking around the group. "Let's move."

Over the next hour, I needed to work as fast as I could with the energy of the Wood and Metal Sigils to create a series of traps. Harper, Daisy, and Caroline kept watch, eyes sharp and ears alert, but I focused on the task at hand.

First, I needed materials.

Keeping my three Sigils – Wood, Metal, and Portal – arranged in my Spirit Grimoire, I sensed the familiar surge of energy course through me. With a flick of my wrist, I summoned the portal to Harrwick. It opened cleanly, a shimmering gateway to the ruined village. I stepped through, surveying the broken remains of the village. Metal scraps littered the area, twisted and jagged from the battle we'd fought there. Perfect for what I needed.

Grabbing as much as I could carry, I stepped back through the portal, depositing the salvaged metal at the base of a tree. With the portal still open, I repeated the process several times, collecting enough material to get started. The rest, I could gather later if needed.

Once I had everything in place, I knelt by the first of the pits Harper had scouted earlier, a natural dip in the ground. Channeling the Wood Sigil, I urged the surrounding roots to twist and bend, forming a solid foundation for the pit. With the Metal Sigil, I shaped long, sharp spikes that lined the bottom, ensuring any goblin that fell in wouldn't be getting back out.

Using my magic, I covered the pit with a thin layer of branches and foliage, carefully arranging it so that it looked like just another patch of underbrush. It only took minutes to create the first spiked pit trap, and I immediately moved on to the next.

While I worked, Harper kept scanning the tree line, his rifle at the ready. "How's it coming?" he asked, his voice low but calm.

"Faster than I thought," I said, not pausing in my efforts. "Shouldn't take much longer than an hour."

He grunted approvingly. "Good. They're still quiet over there, but we can't afford to get sloppy."

Daisy and Caroline were positioned a little farther away, watching the path that led back to the goblin camp. Every so often, Daisy would glance over at me, her eyes tracking my progress with interest. "That portal thing is handy," she muttered, eyes flicking toward the opening to Harrwick.

"You don't know the half of it," I said, already feeling the energy from the Sigils driving me forward.

By the time I'd finished the fifth pit, I was moving even faster. I had the method down. Every pit was deep, lined with spikes, and camouflaged to look like just another patch of forest. Goblins were cunning, but with the traps in place, they wouldn't know what hit them.

Next came the spike traps. Using more of the

salvaged metal, I crafted long spikes, sharp and brutal. These I set into tree trunks and branches, rigging them with tripwires and tension lines made from roots with my Sigil Magic, hidden carefully beneath the leaves and dirt. A single misstep from the goblins, and they'd be impaled before they could even scream. Finally, I shaped funnels, using the Wood Magic to thicken roots and undergrowth to make the most likely paths away from the camp through the trapped areas.

As I shaped the final trap, Harper came over, peering at the work I'd done. "Impressive," he said quietly. "With traps like these, we'll even the odds."

"That's the idea," I said, standing up and brushing off my hands. "We're ready."

Daisy and Caroline returned to our position, both looking relieved. "All quiet so far," Daisy said, her tone a bit more relaxed. "You finish up?"

I nodded. "All done. The traps are in place, and if they don't spot them, we'll have the advantage."

We were all silent for a moment, knowing the time had come to execute our plan. This was a big group of goblins — a real challenge — and there was a chance it would go awry.

But we needed to take the risk.

Chapter 27

We moved into position, each of us taking our designated spots around the encampment. The tension in the air was thick, but we knew what had to be done. Harper crouched to my left, his Garand ready, eyes constantly scanning the goblin camp below. Daisy stood a few paces back, her shotgun raised, waiting. Caroline was further behind, concealed in the brush, keeping an eye on our flank for any surprises.

I tightened my grip on the Mossberg, my pulse steady. The goblins were still unaware of what was coming. We had already laid the groundwork for the funnel, and the traps were set. It was time.

"You sure about this?" Daisy whispered, her eyes flicking toward the camp.

"Trust me. One shot, and they'll come," I said, slipping a shell into the Mossberg. "Just be ready."

She nodded, her eyes sharp. Harper didn't say a word, but the look he gave me said enough. He trusted the plan. Now it was about execution.

I raised the Mossberg, lined up the shot, and aimed for a goblin near the outskirts of the camp. The creature was sharpening a rusted blade, completely oblivious to the danger.

I pulled the trigger.

The shotgun roared, and the goblin's chest exploded in a spray of blood. Chaos erupted instantly. Screeches and guttural howls filled the air as the camp went wild. Goblins grabbed their weapons and began rushing toward the source of the attack — toward me.

I turned and bolted, racing through the trees. Behind me, the goblins' furious shouts grew louder, their footsteps pounding against the ground as they gave chase. They were coming fast, just like we wanted.

I ran straight for the funnel, weaving between trees, jumping over roots, my heart hammering in my chest. The goblins tore through the underbrush, their snarls echoing as they closed in. I darted behind one of the wooden barriers I had created, dropping low, and glanced back just in time to see the first wave of goblins charge into the trap.

The lead goblins hit the tripwires, and a barrage of metal spikes shot out from the trees. The sharp sounds of metal tearing through flesh mixed with the horrific screams as three goblins dropped, impaled by the hidden spikes. Their bodies slumped to the ground, lifeless.

The second wave surged forward, too fast to stop. Two more goblins fell into the first pit, their screams cut short as they were skewered on the spikes lining the bottom. Blood sprayed as they tried to crawl out, but their bodies twitched and went still.

Another goblin triggered a tripwire, and a second set of spikes launched from above, impaling one through the chest. It crumpled to the ground, eyes wide with shock. Behind them, more goblins hesitated, but the ones further back shoved them forward into the killing zone.

Harper fired from his position, picking off another goblin with a single shot to the head. The creature's body jerked violently before it collapsed into the dirt.

Daisy stepped out from cover and unleashed a blast from her shotgun. The goblin she hit flew backward, its chest caving in from the impact. She pumped her shotgun, the sound deafening, and fired again, dropping a second goblin that had scrambled for cover behind a tree.

The remaining goblins were in a frenzy, trying to retreat, but I'd funneled them too well. They couldn't escape. Two more goblins rushed forward, one of them catching a spike to the neck as it stumbled into another tripwire. The last goblin in that group tried to leap over one of the pits, but its foot caught on a root, and it fell hard, impaled on the spikes below.

The screeching grew more desperate as their numbers thinned. Blood stained the ground, and bodies littered the forest floor, but the surviving goblins were far from finished.

Daisy reloaded, her face set in concentration. "There's still more!"

I raised the Mossberg again, taking down a goblin that had managed to avoid the traps. Its body slammed into the dirt with a sickening thud. Caroline shouted a warning from behind as another goblin lunged out of the brush, but Harper was faster. His Garand cracked, and the goblin dropped with a clean shot through its skull.

The remaining goblins finally slowed, realizing the death trap they were in. They stopped running, regrouping near the center of the funnel. There were ten left, snarling, their eyes scanning the forest for the next attack.

We had them cornered, but they weren't finished yet.

The ten remaining goblins grouped up, their yellow eyes scanning the trees, but they had nowhere to run. Harper, Daisy, Caroline, and I exchanged quick looks. It was time to finish this.

"Take them down," I called out.

Harper didn't need any more instructions. He moved with precision, raising his M1 Garand, steadying his aim on the first goblin that looked like it might make a break for it. The rifle cracked, and the goblin dropped, the bullet punching straight through its chest. No hesitation, no wasted motion. Harper was lethal, every shot counting, and I was happy we'd trusted the old man to come along.

Daisy, her shotgun already primed, darted forward, flanking the goblins. She took aim and fired, the blast from the shotgun tearing through a goblin's shoulder. It screeched, spinning to the ground in a heap. She pumped the shotgun again, eyes locked on the next target.

I shifted to the right, my Mossberg raised, and fired at the goblins trying to regroup. One of them took a hit to the torso, its body jerking violently as it was thrown back into the dirt. Another goblin snarled and lunged toward me with a rusted blade in its hand. I turned, taking aim, but Harper's shot rang out before I could pull the trigger, dropping the goblin mid-leap.

"Thanks," I muttered, glancing at Harper as he nodded, his eyes scanning for the next target.

Suddenly, movement to the left caught my attention — one of the goblins had broken off from the group and was sneaking up behind Daisy. She hadn't seen it, too focused on reloading. I couldn't fire, the chance of hitting her was too great.

But one of the branches of the tree that the goblin was about to pass was right next to me.

Without thinking, I reached out with the Wood Sigil, channeling the energy through that branch. At the other end, a root in the goblin's path twisted and sharpened into a series of spikes that jutted up from the ground just in time. The goblin stepped right onto them, its foot pierced by the wooden spikes. It screeched in agony, stumbling and clutching at its leg.

"Daisy!" I shouted.

She spun around, eyes widening for a split second before she reacted. Her shotgun roared, and the goblin's head exploded in a spray of blood. It crumpled, lifeless, the sound of the blast echoing through the trees.

“Nice save!” Daisy called out, giving me a quick nod before turning her attention back to the remaining goblins.

We pressed forward, Harper picking off goblins with expert precision, every shot from his M1 Garand finding its mark. I fired again, the Mossberg bucking in my hands as I took down another goblin, its body collapsing into a pit, disappearing beneath the spikes.

Daisy reloaded and fired again, dropping a goblin that tried to rush her. Its body hit the ground hard, twitching as its lifeblood pooled beneath it.

The last few goblins, seeing their numbers dwindle, tried to make a final stand. They snarled, charging at us with desperate fury. Harper took out another one with a clean headshot, while I pumped my shotgun, aiming at the closest goblin. The blast tore through its chest, sending it spinning into the dirt.

Daisy turned, leveling her shotgun on the final goblin. She fired, the blast ripping through its legs, sending it crashing to the ground. It writhed in pain for a brief moment before going still.

The clearing fell silent, the last of the goblins defeated. Blood and bodies littered the forest floor, the air thick with the acrid scent of gunpowder and death. We stood there for a moment, catching our breath, the adrenaline still pumping through our veins.

"That's all of them," Harper said quietly, lowering his rifle.

Daisy glanced over at me, a grin on her face. "Couldn't have done it without that trick of yours. You saved my butt."

I smiled, breathing a little easier now that the fight was over. "Just glad I was in time."

With the last goblin down, I crouched near its body, wiping the sweat from my brow. The stench of death hung heavy in the air, but there was no time to rest. I quickly began rifling through the goblins' belongings, hoping to find anything of value — information, maybe something they had stolen that could tell us more about their movements.

Nothing.

I checked one corpse after another, turning over

their bodies, sifting through their crude weapons, tattered clothing, and worthless trinkets. Goblins weren't known for their wealth, and these were no exception. Just scraps and filth. I shook my head in frustration, wiping my hands on the grass to rid myself of the grime. Soon after, the corpses faded.

"Find anything?" Harper called out from near the cave entrance. He stood with his rifle ready, eyes scanning the tree line.

I shook my head, standing up. "Nothing useful. Just junk."

Daisy gave a low whistle, still keeping her shotgun close as she joined Harper at the cave. "Figures. They live like animals; they don't keep much around except for whatever they scavenge."

Caroline stood close by, her eyes fixed on the dark opening of the cave. She hadn't said much since the fight ended, but her quiet focus told me enough. I knew her thoughts were ahead — on what might still be lurking in the shadows.

I walked over to them, pulling a flashlight from my pack. The cave mouth yawned open before us, jagged and foreboding. We'd seen them coming and going from here, and if there were more hiding deeper inside, we needed to be sure none were left behind.

"Alright," I said, clicking the flashlight on and illuminating the rocky path ahead. "We're going in. Stay sharp. There could be more waiting in there. Caroline, can you hold the light?"

She nodded and stepped up to take the flashlight. Daisy shifted her shotgun into a more comfortable grip, glancing at me with a wry smile. "Lead the way, boss."

"Let's move," I said, stepping into the darkness, the beam of Caroline's flashlight cutting through the thick gloom of the cave's entrance.

The moment we entered, the temperature dropped, the cool air inside the cave sending a shiver down my spine. The walls were rough and damp, slick with moss and grime. Our footsteps echoed through the narrow passage, boots crunching over loose gravel and dirt. The deeper we went, the more oppressive the air became – thick with the stench of goblin filth. The smell of decay and rot was overwhelming.

"Smells like a damn cesspool in here," Daisy muttered, wrinkling her nose.

I didn't respond, just kept moving forward as Caroline's flashlight revealed more of the winding tunnel ahead. Every twist and turn felt like it could lead to an ambush, the shadows flickering on the uneven walls.

"Watch your step," Harper whispered from behind me. "These tunnels are tight. They could be anywhere."

As we ventured deeper, the sounds around us shifted — soft rustling, the occasional drip of water, and then… something else. A low, guttural snarl echoed through the cave. It was distant but unmistakable, coming from somewhere deeper inside.

I paused, raising my hand to signal the others to stop.

"You hear that?" I asked, my voice low.

They nodded, their expressions tense.

As we moved deeper into the cave, the snarls grew louder, more menacing, echoing off the walls and filling the narrow passage with a sense of impending danger. Caroline's flashlight beam flickered ahead of us, illuminating the jagged rocks and uneven ground. The air felt heavier here, thick with the stench of goblin filth and something more sinister. I could feel it in my bones — something powerful was waiting for us.

"Stay close," I whispered, my voice barely carrying over the low growl in the distance.

Suddenly, the tunnel opened up into a larger chamber, the ceiling high and the walls slick with moisture. At the far end of the room stood a massive goblin, larger and more imposing than any of the others we had faced. Its hunched form loomed in the darkness, but what caught my attention was the staff it held in its gnarled hand — a crude but menacing weapon, pulsing with light.

Embedded in the staff was a *yellow Sigil,* faintly glowing, casting twisted shadows on the walls.

"A Sigil," I muttered.

That was all I had time for before the goblin chief's eyes gleamed with malevolent intelligence, and it raised the staff high, snarling something in its guttural language. As it did, the air around us seemed to shift, and I felt the unmistakable tingle of magic — dark magic.

"Get ready!" I shouted, my grip tightening on

the Mossberg.

Without warning, the goblin chief slammed the staff into the ground, and the Sigil flared to life. A deep rumble echoed through the chamber, and the ceiling above us began to tremble. I looked up just in time to see the rocks shift, cracks spider-webbing across the stone.

"Move!" I shouted, shoving Harper to the side as a massive chunk of rock came crashing down where he had just been standing.

Daisy darted forward, narrowly dodging another falling stone. Caroline yanked the flashlight away, throwing the beam wildly as she dove to the side, barely avoiding the cascade of rubble.

The goblin chief cackled, raising the staff again, clearly intent on bringing the whole chamber down on top of us.

"We've got to take him down, now!" I barked, swinging my Mossberg up and taking aim. Harper was already at my side, his M1 Garand leveled with deadly precision.

As the chief began chanting again, Harper squeezed the trigger, and his rifle cracked sharply, sending a bullet straight toward the goblin. It struck the chief's shoulder, causing it to roar in pain and stagger back. But it wasn't down. Snarling with fury, the chief raised its staff, the yellow Sigil flaring once more.

Rocks began to shake loose again, but this time, I was ready. "Daisy, right!" I yelled, pointing just as another section of the ceiling crumbled above her. She dove, rolling to safety as the stones smashed into the ground.

Harper fired again, this time striking the chief in the chest. The goblin staggered, but the Sigil glowed brighter. I pumped my Mossberg and fired a slug, hitting the chief square in the side.

The goblin chief roared in pain, defiance in its massive frame towering above us. The glow of the yellow Sigil in its staff pulsed wildly, filling the cavern with dark energy. Rocks trembled above, threatening to fall at any moment.

"Caroline, stay back!" I barked, knowing she wasn't equipped to handle this fight. I scooped up some rotting wood and an old scrap of iron. "Hold this!" I stretched out my hand, channeling the Wood and Metal Sigils.

The energy surged through me, and in seconds, I shaped a sturdy shield — crafted from dense wood with reinforced metal edges. It gleamed in the dim light as I passed it to Caroline. "Keep it over Daisy, protect her while she keeps placing shots!"

Caroline nodded, gripping the shield tightly, her eyes wide with determination. She rushed behind Daisy, holding the shield over her as rocks and debris began to rain down.

Harper, already in position, fired. The crack of his M1 Garand echoed through the cavern, and a bullet slammed into the goblin chief's chest. The creature snarled, taking a step back but refusing to go down.

Daisy, shotgun in hand, leveled her sights and fired, the blast catching the chief in the arm. The beast howled, swinging its staff wildly. The ceiling groaned, more rocks falling, but Caroline was quick, holding the shield steady, protecting Daisy from the debris.

"We've got to break through that thick hide!" Harper shouted, reloading with precision, firing another shot aimed directly at the chief's head.

The bullet grazed its ear, drawing blood but still not enough to stop it.

I focused, channeling more of the Wood Sigil. The roots and vines in the cave responded, creeping along the walls and wrapping around the chief's legs, trying to slow it down. The creature struggled, snarling as it raised its staff again. The Sigil flared, sending a shockwave of magic through the chamber, dislodging more stones and shattering part of the ceiling.

"Daisy, now!" I yelled, ducking beneath a falling chunk of rock.

Daisy didn't hesitate. She fired again, this time hitting the chief in the gut. The goblin stumbled, its grip on the staff loosening for a moment. Harper took advantage, firing another shot, this time striking the chief in the shoulder, causing it to roar in pain.

The Sigil flared one last time. The goblin raised its staff, clearly desperate, summoning another wave of rocks from above. But I wasn't about to let that happen. With a final surge of energy, I darted forward and raised my Mossberg. The weapon cracked, and the slug pierced through the creature's chest with a sickening crunch.

The goblin let out a strangled cry, its staff falling from its grasp as it crumpled to its knees. The glow of the yellow Sigil flickered, then dimmed, leaving only the sound of the creature's labored breaths.

I stepped forward, my Mossberg aimed at its head. "Die," I said coldly, pulling the trigger.

The blast echoed through the chamber, and the goblin chief collapsed, lifeless. The Sigil on its staff flickered one final time before going dark. The room fell eerily quiet, save for the sound of dust and rocks settling.

Harper lowered his rifle, breathing heavily, and Daisy wiped the sweat from her brow. Caroline, still holding the shield, let out a long breath of relief, her eyes meeting mine.

The goblin chief was dead.

Chapter 28

We stood in the stillness of the cave, the only sound the soft patter of debris settling from the battle. I lowered my Mossberg, taking a steadying breath as I surveyed the scene while the ringing in my ears slowly subsided. The goblin chief lay dead at our feet, its hulking form crumpled in the dirt. The glow of the Sigil embedded in its staff had faded, leaving only the dull, twisted wood and metal in its hand.

"Good work," Harper muttered, reloading his M1 Garand with practiced ease. "That thing was no joke."

Daisy stretched her arms, rolling her neck. "Damn straight. We've seen some ugly goblins before, but that one... he takes the cake."

Caroline stepped forward cautiously, her eyes wide as she scanned the cave walls. "What now?"

I knelt beside the goblin chief's body, my attention fixed on the staff. The Sigil embedded within it might have been dormant now, but I could still sense its power. This wasn't just some crude goblin weapon — it was crafted with purpose, likely scavenged from somewhere far beyond this cave.

Carefully, I pried the staff from the creature's gnarled fingers, feeling the weight of the wood and the cold metal banding wrapped around it. The Sigil was dim, but it still pulsed faintly beneath my touch — a yellow glow that told me it had more to offer. It came to me almost at once, as if some unearthly force placed the knowledge in my mind.

"It's a Magnetic Sigil," I said, holding the staff up for the others to see. "That's how the chief was able to pull down those rocks. It's powerful, and if I can unlock its full potential, it could be useful."

Daisy eyed it warily. "Think it's safe to mess with?"

"Well, I wouldn't 'mess' with magic, but if it's like the other Sigils, I can control it."

As I stood, I took in the rest of the chamber. The cave was littered with all sorts of crude objects – broken tools, twisted bits of metal, and piles of stolen goods that the goblins had hoarded over the years. Most of it was junk, but some pieces stood out, old relics clearly taken from human settlements. It seemed they had been here for a while.

"Spread out," I said, nodding toward the piles. "See if there's anything valuable."

We moved carefully through the debris, sifting through the mess. Harper kicked over a rusted pot, grunting when nothing useful fell out. Daisy crouched by a pile of discarded weapons, most of which were too rusted to be of any use. But it was

Caroline who spotted something first.

"Over here," she called softly, her fingers brushing against a small, weathered box tucked beneath a pile of broken crates.

I joined her, kneeling beside the box. It was old — really old. The wood was splintered and worn, the metal hinges rusted with age. But when I pulled the lid open, it revealed something unexpected: a collection of items that must have dated back to the 19th century. Inside, there were tarnished silverware, an intricately carved pocket watch, and what looked like a small locket, all clearly human-made.

"These have been here a long time," Caroline murmured, picking up the locket. "How did goblins even get their hands on these?"

I shook my head. "Could've been stolen from settlers, or even travelers who came through this area a century ago. These goblins seem to hoard whatever they find."

As she set the locket down, Caroline's gaze shifted to something else in the box — a book, its leather cover cracked with age but surprisingly well-preserved. She carefully lifted it out, her eyes widening as she brushed away the dust.

"A journal," she said softly, opening it to the first page. The writing was faded but still legible, the neat cursive script dated over a hundred years ago. "I'll take this back with me, see if I can make sense of it later."

I nodded. "Good idea. Anything that can give us a better understanding of the history here might be valuable." As the girls and Harper gathered it all up, I stood in the cave, turning the goblin chief's staff in my hand, feeling the faint pulse of the Magnetic Sigil embedded within it.

There was power here, and I was itching to see what it could do.

"I want to try something," I said, glancing at the others.

Daisy smirked, leaning casually on her shotgun. "You've always got somethin' up your sleeve. What is it this time?"

I chuckled, setting the staff aside and crouching down to sift through the junk scattered across the cave floor. My hand closed around a rusty old axe, the blade dull and useless. "Greida gave me a new slot in the Spirit Grimoire. I'm going to combine this Magnetic Sigil with the Metal Sigil and see what happens."

Caroline stepped closer, eyes bright with curiosity. "You're going to use both Sigils together? Can you even do that?"

"Only one way to find out," I replied with a grin. "Watch."

Closing my eyes, I pictured the Spirit Grimoire in my mind. The Sigils glowed softly on the pages, their power waiting to be used. I focused on the Magnetic Sigil first, drawing its energy toward me. A hum of power surged through me as I guided the Sigil into the new slot Greida had granted. The energy swirled, merging smoothly with my Spirit Grimoire as the material version of the Magnetic Sigil disappeared. Next, I moved the Metal Sigil to combine with it, leaving the Wood and Portal Sigil in the first Spirit Grimoire slot.

I felt the new connection lock into place, the two Sigils now joined and ready.

A faint glow appeared around the axe in my hand as the Sigils absorbed into the Grimoire. The moment the energy settled, I knew what I wanted to do.

"Alright," I said, standing. I held the axe out in front of me, focusing on the rusty head. The Metal Sigil responded, the rust flaking off as I manipulated the material. "Let's see how this works."

Harper, who had been silently watching from the entrance, gave a nod. "Show us."

I concentrated, and the metal of the axe head began to unravel, transforming into dozens of tiny, sharp nails. They floated in the air around me, suspended by the force of the Magnetic Sigil. I smiled at the sight, then extended my hand, palm outward. The nails shot forward in a burst of magnetic energy, embedding themselves in the far cave wall with a series of sharp *thunks*.

"Well, I'll be damned," Harper said, lowering his rifle. "That's one hell of a trick."

Daisy's jaw dropped. "Did you just... turn an axe into a nail gun? That there is badassed!"

I grinned, lowering my hand as the energy from the Sigils faded. "Looks like it worked."

Caroline, wide-eyed, stepped closer to the wall where the nails had embedded. "That was incredible. You just... reshaped the metal and launched it with the Sigil's magnetic power?"

"Exactly," I said. "The Magnetic Sigil made it possible to direct them like that."

Daisy nudged me playfully. "Forget makin' traps — I need you to whip me up one of those for next time we're out hunting."

I laughed. "We'll see what I can do."

With nothing else of value left in the goblin's camp, we made our way out of the cave, each of us on high alert despite the silence that had settled in after the battle. The goblin chief's body had already begun to fade, just like the others, but the presence of the Magnetic Sigil still pulsed faintly in the back of my mind, the Sigil itself safely absorbed into my Spirit Grimoire.

Harper glanced around, his sharp eyes scanning the tree line. "Looks like we've wiped out the lot of them," he muttered. "This'll keep the town and your home safe for a while. Hopefully, there are no more of the little bastards around."

I nodded. He had a point, of course. There could be more goblins, more camps. There wasn't a guarantee that this was all. And then there was that troll still skulking in the forest. Taking that down would require a careful plan, like with the one we killed at Harrwick. Still, with the Magnetic Sigil, there were now a lot more options.

I smiled and nodded to myself, feeling better equipped to deal with whatever was coming. I threw a satisfied look at my companions – brave Daisy, smart Caroline, and the crafty old Harper. "Well done, everyone," I said. "I think we took control of this whole situation today!"

Daisy slung her shotgun over her shoulder, grinning as she took a deep breath of the cool, fresh air. "Yeah, that feels good! Those little bastards were dug in deep, but we cleaned 'em out. Feels like a job well done."

Caroline, quiet as always, walked beside us, though I could tell from the way her eyes darted around that she wasn't letting her guard down just yet. "It was smart, the way they used that cave," she said softly. "They had the perfect hiding spot, but now it's over."

"Yeah, it is," I said, glancing back at the entrance one last time. A major threat had been neutralized, and with that gone, I felt a weight lift from my shoulders. The goblins wouldn't be bothering us again anytime soon. But the troll was still out there — somewhere. And it wasn't the kind of problem that would just disappear.

We moved cautiously through the forest, Harper leading the way with his rifle still at the ready. Even though the danger had passed, there was always the chance of stragglers or other creatures drawn by the noise of the battle. But the woods were quiet now, the only sound the occasional rustling of leaves in the wind.

As we made our way back to the edge of the forest, my thoughts drifted to Brooke. This was the kind of threat I wanted her and Cody far away from, and now that the goblins were gone, I could breathe a little easier. But the troll remained. I needed to deal with that sooner rather than later if I wanted Brooke to feel comfortable enough to spend more time out here.

I glanced at Harper, who was scanning the tree line like always. "We've bought ourselves some time," I said. "But the troll… that's still hanging over us. I need to take care of it before it gets bold enough to come any closer."

Harper grunted, nodding. "You've got the right idea. Trolls are a different beast, though. You'll need more than just traps to deal with that one."

"I know," I said. "But I'll find a way. I have to."

Daisy, walking beside me, gave me a sideways glance. "You think Brooke's gonna come around more now? I reckon she's warming up to the idea of sticking around. And with them goblins gone, I reckon it's safer, right?"

"I hope so," I replied, feeling that familiar warmth when I thought about her. "We'll see. I think Cody's got a lot to do with it. He loves it here. I just need to show her that it's safe. That I've got everything under control."

"And you do," Caroline added, her voice steady and calm. "You've done more than enough to keep us all safe."

We reached the edge of the forest, where my truck was parked. The sun was just beginning to dip below the horizon, casting long shadows across the landscape. As we loaded up, I looked back at the dark trees one last time. The goblin threat was gone, but there were more challenges out there, and I had to be ready.

But for now, we'd earned a bit of peace.

Harper climbed into the bed of the truck with a satisfied grunt, while Daisy and Caroline settled in beside me in the cab. I glanced over at them with a smile. "We'll head back to the house, take a breather, and then figure out our next move," I said.

Daisy shot me a grin. "Sounds like a plan."

With that, I started the engine, and we drove off, leaving the forest and its dangers behind — for now.

Chapter 29

After dropping Harper off and pulling back up to the house, I stepped out of the truck, greeted by the sound of Tink's eager bark. The smell of a home-cooked meal hit me the second I opened the door, and my stomach growled in response. Daisy and Caroline were already at work in the kitchen, but the easy laughter coming from inside made it feel like I was walking into exactly the place I wanted to be.

I kicked off my boots by the door, the sights and smells of my cozy home grounding me after the long day. "Something smells damn good," I called out, making my way into the kitchen.

Daisy turned from the stove, spoon in hand, and smirked. "Yup, yup! Told you I had dinner covered, didn't I? Stew's almost ready, so don't get too excited yet."

Caroline looked up from setting the table, a soft smile on her lips. "It's mostly Daisy. I just... did some of the potatoes."

"Don't be modest," Daisy teased, giving her a playful nudge with her elbow. "You've got the touch, sweetie. You've been helpin' out!"

Caroline blushed, brushing a strand of ginger hair behind her ear. "I just followed your directions."

I stepped up behind Daisy, peeking over her shoulder at the pot of stew simmering on the stove. "That's how you learn. Smells incredible. You keep this up, and I'm going to be useless in the kitchen."

Daisy shot me a grin. "Aren't you already?" she teased, bumping me with her luscious hips.

I chuckled, leaning against the counter. "I can cook. Might not be as fancy as whatever magic you're stirring up, but I won't starve."

"Uh-huh," Daisy said, giving the stew one last stir before pulling the pot off the stove. "We'll see about that. But tonight? You just sit your pretty behind down and enjoy."

Caroline was already placing the bread on the table, glancing my way. "I think we've earned it, right? A little rest after today?"

"Definitely earned it," I said, grabbing a plate. "Kicking goblin ass works up an appetite."

Daisy chuckled, dishing out generous servings of stew into bowls. "You and me both."

We sat down at the table, the three of us digging into the meal like it was the best thing we'd had in weeks. The stew was perfect — rich, savory, with just the right amount of spices. The bread that the girls served with it was warm and soft. It was the kind of meal that made you feel like you were right where you needed to be.

"Wow, Daisy," I said after taking my first bite.

"This is incredible. Seriously, I don't know how you do it."

Daisy leaned back, clearly enjoying the compliment. "Like I said — years of practice. You want a real meal? You come to me. I'll take care of you." She winked. "In more ways than one, too..."

I grinned and shook my head as Caroline looked between the two of us. "It really is good. I think this is exactly what we needed after today."

Daisy nodded, her eyes sparkling. "Right? There's nothing like a full belly after a fight. You know, back when I lived on the farm, this was the kind of thing we'd make after a long day in the fields. You eat something like this, and it makes all the hard work worth it."

Caroline smiled. "I can see why. I've never had anything like this."

"You're doing just fine for yourself," I said, giving her a nod. "This stew are perfect. You're picking this up fast."

Caroline blushed again, shaking her head. "I just... followed Daisy's lead. She's the one who made the meal."

Daisy wagged her spoon at Caroline. "Hey, no

more of that. You helped, and that's what matters. Don't sell yourself short."

Caroline looked down, then glanced up at us, her expression shifting. "I appreciate that, but... I don't know. Today, out there? I felt a little... useless."

I stopped mid-chew. "Useless? No way, Caroline. You did exactly what you were supposed to do. Kept watch, stayed alert. You were part of the team."

"Damn right!" Daisy agreed.

Caroline let out a soft sigh, her gaze falling back to her plate. "But that's just it. I wasn't... doing anything. Not like you or Daisy or Harper. I was just *there,* watching. I want to do more. I want to learn how to defend myself."

I leaned forward, locking eyes with her. "Caroline, listen to me. You weren't useless out there. You kept your head, and you made sure we didn't get flanked. That's not 'just watching.' That's keeping us alive."

Daisy nodded, her voice firmer. "Yeah. You think I could've focused on shootin' those goblins if I didn't know you had our backs? Hell no. And don't forget, you were the one keeping me safe with that shield Sean whipped up. Reckon I'd be squashed right now if you hadn't been there."

Caroline looked up, her eyes wide. "I... didn't really think of it that way."

I gave her a reassuring smile. "Well, that's how it was. But if you want to learn how to defend yourself, I'll teach you. There's no rush, and we'll take it slow. But you're part of this team, Caroline. We need you."

She hesitated for a moment, then gave a small nod, her expression softening. "I'd like that. I just don't want to be the one who always needs saving."

Daisy reached across the table, squeezing Caroline's hand. "You're holding your own just fine, Caroline," she said.

Caroline's smile grew a little wider, a spark of confidence lighting in her eyes. "I guess you're right. I just... I don't want to hold anyone back."

"You're not," I said. "You're helping more than you realize. And when you're ready, we'll start training. But don't ever think you're not pulling your weight, Caroline."

She nodded again, a quiet determination settling into her expression. "Okay. I'll take you up on that training offer. I want to be ready for whatever comes next."

Daisy grinned, lifting her glass. "That's the spirit. To kickin' ass and takin' names, right?"

Caroline laughed softly, lifting her own glass. "Right."

We clinked our glasses together, the mood lightening as the conversation shifted. We talked about the fight, recounting the details with more laughter than tension now that we were on the other side of it.

As the plates emptied and the night wore on, I felt a deep sense of contentment settle over me. This — sitting around a table, sharing a meal and laughing — was what I fought for. The battles were hard, and there would always be more, but as long as we could celebrate our victories together, I'd happily face the world with these women at my side.

The only people missing were Brooke and Cody. But deep down inside, I had a feeling they might soon join us here, too.

After dinner, we stayed around the table, enjoying the lingering warmth of the meal and the easy conversation.

I leaned back, nursing my drink while Daisy and Caroline kept up their usual banter. It was the kind of moment where you didn't want to move, the time when laughter comes easy, and the weight of the day has already started to fade.

Daisy, ever quick to stir things up, grinned at Caroline and gave her a playful nudge. "You know, Caroline, you surprised me out there today. Didn't know you had that kind of calm in you."

Caroline blushed lightly, adjusting her glasses as she smiled. "I didn't feel calm. I thought my heart was going to pound out of my chest."

"Could've fooled me," Daisy shot back, laughing. "You looked like you were holding it together better than most tough guys I know." She shot me a teasing wink. "Maybe better than Sean, even."

I smirked. "Oh, is that right? I didn't hear anyone complaining when I saved your ass from that goblin, Daisy."

Daisy waved her hand dismissively, obviously enjoying my teasing her back a little. "Pfft. One goblin. Please. I was about to handle it myself."

Caroline giggled at the back-and-forth. "You weren't about to handle anything. You didn't even see it coming."

"See? Even Caroline's got your number," I said, grinning.

Daisy rolled her eyes, but her grin didn't falter. "Yeah, yeah. Keep givin' me a hard time. Next time, I'll let the goblin have a shot at you before I step in and save the day."

"Sounds fair," I said with a chuckle. "We'll see who's saving who."

Caroline shook her head, her smile still in place. "I think you both did fine. And for the record, I wasn't as calm as you think. I was mostly just trying not to panic."

Daisy leaned in, her voice dropping conspiratorially. "You say that, but you were cool under pressure. I noticed. You didn't flinch once. Maybe next time we'll see you take down a goblin or two. I'm telling you, sister: you got the makings of a warrior!"

Caroline laughed, but it was soft, almost shy. "I don't know about that," she just hummed softly.

I raised an eyebrow. "You're selling yourself short. You did better than you realize."

Caroline shrugged, glancing at me. "Maybe. But I definitely need more practice before I'd ever feel comfortable jumping into a fight."

"You'll get there, sweet plums," Daisy said confidently. "You've got the brains, Caroline. You just need the confidence to match. Stick with us, and we'll make sure you're ready for anything."

"That's the plan," I added, nodding. "No rush. But when you're ready, we'll make sure you know what you're doing."

We fell into a comfortable rhythm, trading more stories about the fight. After a few minutes of banter, Daisy leaned back in her chair, stretching her arms above her head with a satisfied sigh. "You know, there's something I've been thinkin' 'bout for a while now."

I raised an eyebrow. "Oh yeah? What's that?"

Daisy gave me a knowing grin, her eyes glinting with mischief. "Well... I've got a pretty strong suspicion that we weren't alone the other night."

Caroline blinked, looking confused. "What do you mean?"

Daisy's grin widened as she turned to me. "I mean, I'm pretty sure Brooke was watching the three of us when we were… well, you know…"

Caroline's eyes went wide, her cheeks flushing bright red. "Wait, what?! She was watching?"

I couldn't help but laugh at the sudden shift in tone, shaking my head as I met Daisy's playful gaze. "Not confirming or denying anything here."

Daisy's grin didn't falter. "Oh, come on. You can't tell me you didn't notice."

Caroline, still reeling from the comment, looked between us, her face a mix of shock and disbelief. "She was... watching? Are you serious?"

Daisy nodded, clearly enjoying herself. "I mean, think about it. We were makin' a little noise, y'know? She heard. You really think she could resist sneakin' a peek?"

Caroline's blush deepened, and she buried her face in her hands. "Oh my God, this is too much."

I chuckled, shaking my head. "Look, I'm not saying she did or didn't."

Caroline peeked out from behind her hands, still

blushing furiously. "I can't believe you two are just casually talking about this."

Daisy shrugged, leaning back in her chair like she didn't have a care in the world. "Why not? We're all adults here, right? Brooke's a grown woman. She's allowed to be curious."

Caroline laughed, though it was muffled by her hands. "This is so embarrassing."

Daisy grinned even wider. "You know what's even better? I bet she liked what she saw. Hell, if I were her, I'd wanna jump right in."

I raised my glass, smirking. "Like I said, I'm not confirming or denying anything."

Caroline looked at me, her eyes wide. "Wait... it sounds like you are you saying she actually *did* watch?"

I shrugged, still smiling. "I'm just saying Brooke's got her own mind. What she chooses to do with her curiosity is up to her."

Daisy laughed, clearly enjoying how flustered Caroline had gotten. "You see? This is why I love Sean. He's got that 'strong, silent type' thing down pat. Never gives too much away, but you know there's always more goin' on."

Caroline shook her head, laughing despite her embarrassment. "I can't believe I'm even listening to this."

Daisy leaned in, her voice dropping to a playful whisper. "You want to know what I think? I think she was glued to the scene, just listening and wishin' she could be part of it." She licked her lips and rubbed her thighs together, her own talk obviously getting her a little riled up. "No way she wasn't at least curious."

Caroline stifled a laugh, her face still bright red. "This conversation is ridiculous."

Daisy winked at her. "Ridiculously fun, you mean."

Caroline covered her face with her hands again, laughing softly. "Okay, maybe a little."

I chuckled, watching the two of them go back and forth. "If Brooke ever decides to join, that'll be her call. But I think she enjoyed the show in her own way."

Caroline peeked out from behind her hands again, her smile softening as she glanced at me. "I doubt she'd have the courage to actually... *join*."

Daisy gave her a knowing look. "Oh, I don't

know. Brooke seems like the adventurous type. We might have her with us sooner or later."

Caroline laughed, clearly still trying to wrap her head around the idea. "Well, I'm definitely not going to be the one to bring it up."

I grinned, leaning back in my chair. "Don't worry, Caroline. I'll handle that conversation if it ever comes up."

Daisy burst out laughing, raising her glass in mock celebration. "To Brooke, and to Sean handling all the delicate conversations!"

Caroline shook her head, though she couldn't stop herself from laughing. "You two are impossible."

"And you love it," Daisy shot back, winking at her.

Caroline smiled, finally relaxing as the laughter and teasing continued to flow. The mood between us had shifted into something light, flirty, and fun, and I could tell that Caroline was starting to let go of her embarrassment, embracing the playful energy we shared.

Daisy raised her glass again, her eyes glinting with mischief. "Here's to a wild night. And next time... maybe Brooke gets a front-row seat."

"A wild night, huh?" I said, eyebrow perked.

"Hm-hm," Daisy hummed, her blue eyes sparkling with mischief. "In fact, Caroline and I got ourselves a little plan for this evening." She exchanged a mysterious glance with Caroline, who responded with a coy smile.

"Really?" I asked, raising an eyebrow, intrigued. "What kind of plan?"

Daisy grinned, revealing nothing. "You'll find out soon enough. Just give us ten minutes, and then come to the bedroom, alright?" She stood up, Caroline in tow, and they giggled all the way upstairs, leaving me alone in the living room.

Chapter 30

I couldn't help but chuckle as my two girls headed upstairs. My curiosity was certainly piqued. What were those two up to? They knew how to keep me on my toes. I felt a pleasant fluttering in my stomach as I listened to the faint sound of giggling from above.

Time seemed to crawl by, and my anticipation

grew, my heart racing with each tick of the clock. Finally, after what felt like an agonizingly long wait, the ten-minute mark arrived.

Grinning, I made my way upstairs, my pulse quickening as I tried to imagine what awaited me behind that closed door. As I approached the door to the master bedroom, I could still hear their muffled laughter, only adding to the mystery surrounding their plan.

Taking a deep breath, I raised my hand and knocked gently on the door. "Ladies, may I come in?"

"Come on in, Sean!" Caroline called out, sounding both excited and slightly nervous.

I opened the door, and it revealed a vision that nearly took my breath away.

There they were, Caroline and Daisy, sprawled out on the massive bed in the most enticing lingerie I'd ever seen — stockings and garter belts clinging to their shapely legs, thongs leaving little to the imagination, and skimpy see-through bras barely containing their ample breasts.

My lust surged like a tidal wave, threatening to sweep me under.

"Come on in, sugar," Daisy said as she beckoned me closer. Her curvy figure was accentuated by the lace and silk that adorned her body, making it impossible for me to tear my gaze away.

"Whoa," I stammered, stepping into the room, my heart pounding in my chest. "You two look... incredible."

"Thank you, Sean," Caroline replied. "We wanted to give you a little surprise tonight."

Her green eyes met mine, her voluptuous form wrapped in the same seductive attire as Daisy's. The sight of them both, laid out before me like an offering, was almost too much to bear.

But as I moved to join them, Daisy raised a hand, halting my progress. "Hold up there, cowboy," she said with a grin. "We ain't quite ready for you yet."

My brow furrowed, but I decided to humor them. Standing there, I crossed my arms and waited. "Alright," I said. "Don't know if I'll hold out for long, though."

"Won't take long," Daisy purred.

Then, I watched intently as Daisy rolled onto

her smooth stomach, her firm, tanned ass now on full display in its skimpy thong. And in a vision straight from heaven, Caroline reached for a bottle of oil, uncapping it with a soft pop.

She began drizzling the slick liquid over Daisy's butt cheeks, the oily sheen catching the low light in the room, making her skin glow.

"You two are driving me crazy," I said, unable to hide the arousal in my voice. "What's the plan here?"

Daisy glanced back at me over her shoulder, a wicked smile playing on her lips. "Well, darlin', I couldn't help but notice how much fun you had with Caroline's pretty little butt the other night," she confessed, her cheeks flushing a delicate pink. "And I gotta admit... I'm more than a little curious to try it myself."

Well, damn…

My eyes widened at her admission, the thought of taking Daisy in such an intimate way sending a shiver down my spine.

As I stood there, Caroline hopped out of the bed, and in an ultimate moment of fantasy, she crawled over to me on all fours, and I couldn't help but chuckle.

"You two are crazy," I said. "I love it."

Caroline licked her lips and kept her green lookers on me as her fingers deftly undid each button on my shirt, her green eyes never leaving mine. Behind her, Daisy was spreading the oil over her tanned cheeks, her thong pulled aside to reveal a heart-shaped butt plug nestled between them.

Damn again…

"You know, baby," Daisy said, her voice husky. "I've been wearin' this all evening, just thinkin' 'bout what we'd be doin' tonight."

"Is that so?" I asked, my breath hitching as Caroline slid my pants down my legs, exposing my throbbing erection.

"Uh-huh." She flashed me a sultry smile before turning her attention back to the task at hand.

With my clothes discarded in a heap beside the bed, Caroline sank to her knees and wrapped her full lips around my cock. The warmth of her mouth, coupled with the sight of Daisy lubricating her ass, sent shivers of pleasure down my spine. Caroline sucked hard and fast, her hands gripping my thighs for support as she took me deeper.

"Are you ready, baby?" Daisy called out, her fingers removing the plug from her well-prepped entrance.

"More than ready," I replied, my voice hoarse with desire.

"Then come here," she beckoned, a hint of nervousness in her beautiful eyes. This was exciting for her — and for me too.

Caroline licked her lips before she spat on my cock, providing extra lubrication, and gave me an encouraging nod. My lust nearly overpowering, I stepped forward onto the bed and kissed Daisy passionately. Her body trembled beneath my touch.

"I... uh... I ain't ever done this before," she admitted, biting her lip. "Be gentle, baby."

"Tell me how you want it," I urged, wanting her to be comfortable.

"Would you... would you lie down so I can sit on you?" she suggested. She bit her lip. "That... that seems really hot to me."

"Of course, whatever makes you comfortable," I replied before kissing her. She kissed back passionately, losing herself already, and she pushed me down onto the bed with a playful grin.

As I lay down, my gaze was locked onto her in her tantalizing lingerie and stockings, her thong pulled to the side. The sight of her straddling me with her backside facing me sent a jolt of excitement through my body. Her perfect curves were accentuated by the skimpy outfit as she settled into a reverse cowgirl position.

"Let me help you," Caroline purred, joining us on the bed.

I smiled at her as she took hold of my cock, guiding it towards Daisy's tight entrance. The warmth of Caroline's hand and the anticipation of what was to come made me dizzy with desire.

"Thanks, sweetie," Daisy said to Caroline, her voice breathy and excited.

"Anything for you two," Caroline replied with a warm smile.

Daisy let out a gentle moan as she began to lower herself onto my cock. My heart raced as I felt her tight opening envelop me, sending waves of pleasure coursing through my body. It was an intoxicating sensation, one that left me reeling with delight.

"Ah, Sean... you feel so good," Daisy whimpered, her body trembling with pleasure.

"God, you're so tight, Daisy," I groaned, unable to contain my own excitement.

Caroline leaned in close, whispering seductively in my ear, "This is so incredibly hot." As she spoke, her free hand wandered down the front of her own thong, seeking her own pleasure amidst our shared experience.

"You… Hmm… you are makin' me feel amazing," Daisy murmured.

The sensation of Daisy's tightness wrapped around me was overwhelming, and I bit my lip to keep from losing myself completely in the moment. With each slow, deliberate movement of her hips, the pleasure intensified, leaving me breathless and desperate for more.

"God, Sean," Daisy drawled, her voice seductively husky. "I never felt anythin' like this before. Hmmm… Your cock feels incredible in my ass."

As she continued to gently ride me, I reached up, my hands finding purchase on her firm, tanned butt cheeks. My thumbs pressed into the dimples at the small of her back, helping to guide her movements as she began to grow more confident.

"Uh, Daisy... you're so sexy like this... it's amazing," I managed to gasp out, my breath ragged with desire.

Caroline, not content to simply watch, took the opportunity to release her voluptuous breasts from the confines of her skimpy bra. Leaning over, she pressed her freckled mounds against my face.

I eagerly kissed her breasts, my tongue tracing circles around her erect nipples as I savored the taste of her soft, freckled skin.

"Damn, y'all are so hot together," Daisy purred as she looked over her shoulder while riding my dick with her tight ass. With a lustful moan, she began to pick up the pace of her movements as she reached around to spread her ass cheeks, allowing me to sink even deeper inside her. "I can feel you goin' so deep, Sean... it's drivin' me wild!"

Feeling bolder now, Daisy leaned back, her fingers finding her own clit as she continued to bounce on my throbbing cock. Her dirty talk grew even more intense, the words spilling from her lips like a sultry mantra.

"You two are makin' me so wet, I can barely stand it," she moaned, her fingers working furiously. "Sean, your cock feels so good in my ass..."

"God, Daisy, you're incredible," I gasped out between licks and sucks on Caroline's sensitive nipples. "Keep going... I want to see you lose yourself completely."

Caroline's breath hitched as she watched us, her own pleasure mounting. "This is so hot... it's making me cum... I can't hold back any longer," she panted, her voice straining with ecstasy.

Her breathing grew more ragged. She was getting closer and closer to the edge. "Oh, Sean... I'm gonna cum," she moaned, her fingers working feverishly between her legs.

"Cum for me," I urged her, my tongue flicking over her sensitive nipple. "Let it all out."

And with a shuddering gasp, Caroline finally surrendered to her orgasm. Her body trembled as waves of pleasure washed over her, and I felt her nails dig into my scalp, holding me close. Her moans filled the room, echoing off the walls in a symphony of ecstasy.

"Damn, that's so hot, Caroline," Daisy breathed from above me, her hips still rocking back and forth as she rode my cock. The sight of Caroline's climax seemed to push her over the edge as well, and I could feel her body tense up around me. "I'm gonna cum too... Oh God, Sean, it feels so good!"

"Cum for me, baby," I encouraged her, biting my lip as her ass began bouncing faster on my cock. My own orgasm was rapidly approaching, but I held onto my control with an iron grip, determined to let these two incredible women have their moment first.

Daisy's eyes squeezed shut and she cried out, her climax hitting her like a tidal wave. As she came, her muscles clenched tightly around my shaft, sending electric jolts of pleasure through me. I fought to keep my composure, but it was growing increasingly difficult.

"Sean..." Daisy panted, still in the throes of her orgasm. "Please... I want you to cum in my ass... Give it to me."

Caroline, still catching her breath, added her own plea. "Do it, Sean... Give Daisy what she wants."

It was too much for me to resist any longer. My fingers dug into the soft flesh of Daisy's ass cheeks as I pulled her down hard, burying myself as deep inside her as I could go. With a guttural growl, I let go and released my seed into her tight, welcoming heat.

The sensation was indescribable – like a supernova exploding within me, radiating waves of pleasure through every nerve and fiber of my body. As my orgasm subsided, I felt a sense of euphoria wash over me, leaving me completely spent.

Exhausted and breathless, Daisy collapsed on top of me, her body still trembling from the intensity of our shared climax.

Caroline, equally spent, fell onto the bed beside me, her chest heaving as she tried to catch her breath. The room was filled with the scent of sex and sweat.

"Damn," Daisy muttered. "That was… easily the hottest thing I've ever done."

Caroline giggled, her eyes sparkling with mischief and pride in her own role in our erotic escapade. "I knew you'd like it, Daisy," she said.

I felt my heart swell with love for these two incredible women who had brought such pleasure into my life. The warmth of their bodies pressed against mine was a delight of its own, and as I basked in the afterglow, I couldn't help but wonder if there could ever be anything better than this — lying here, spent and satisfied, with the two people I cared for most in the world.

"Come here," I murmured, pulling them both close so that their heads rested on my chest. They snuggled in without hesitation, their soft sighs and gentle touches further deepening the bond between us.

"You really know how to make a girl feel good," Daisy whispered, her words muffled by my skin as she nuzzled against me. "Ain't nothin' quite like this, is there?"

"No," I agreed, my voice barely more than a whisper as I stroked their hair. "This is the best."

As we lay there, entwined together in the dim light, I couldn't help but think about how incredibly lucky I was to have found not just one, but two soulmates who understood me, loved me, and brought me such indescribable joy.

And as sleep began to claim us, our bodies tangled together in a mess of limbs and contented sighs, I drifted off happily, hoping many more nights like this one would follow.

Chapter 31

I woke up slowly, feeling the warmth of Daisy and Caroline beside me, their soft breaths the only sound in the quiet room. I glanced over at them, both still fast asleep. Daisy was curled into me, her arm draped lazily over my waist, while Caroline rested her head against my shoulder. I smiled at the sight, not wanting to disturb them. Carefully, I slid out of bed, making sure not to wake either of them.

As I tiptoed downstairs, I felt a sense of peace. After everything we'd been through lately — the goblins, the fights, even my struggles with the Sigils — it felt like things were finally starting to fall into place. I was getting a better grip on my magic, the house was safe again, and for now, everything was calm. It was a good feeling — one I wasn't used to but welcomed all the same.

Reaching the kitchen, I started the coffee, the quiet hum of the machine filling the silence. I leaned back against the counter, thinking about what was next. We'd handled the goblins, but I still had the troll to deal with. That was going to be a whole different fight, one I'd have to prepare for. But with the new Magnetic Sigil, I felt ready, more in control than I had been in a long time.

My phone buzzed on the counter, pulling me out of my thoughts. I glanced at the screen — Brooke. I answered immediately, sensing something was off.

"Hey, Brooke. What's going on?"

Her voice came through, shaky and strained.

"Sean… I — I don't know what to do. I'm at work, and I've been here all night, and… I just feel like I'm losing it."

I straightened up, immediately on alert. "Slow down. What happened?"

"I got caught up in this huge project. I didn't mean to, but I just kept going and going, and now it's morning, and I haven't slept, and Cody's with the sitter, and I just… I can't keep doing this, Sean." Her voice cracked, and I could hear the exhaustion and panic creeping in.

"Okay," I said softly, trying to keep my voice steady for her sake. "Take a deep breath for me, alright? I'm here."

She was quiet for a second, and I could hear her taking a shaky breath. "I just… I don't know how it got so bad. I told myself I'd leave by midnight, but then the emails kept coming in, and my phone wouldn't stop buzzing, and now I feel like I'm drowning. I don't even know where to start."

"Alright, listen," I said, keeping my tone calm and firm. "You don't have to figure it all out right now. Where are you? Still at the office?"

"Yeah," she said, her voice small. "I didn't even

leave. I've been here all night."

"Okay. First thing, you need to get out of there. Can you head home? I'll meet you there."

"Sean, you don't have to do that. I can handle it, I just—"

"No," I cut in, shaking my head even though she couldn't see me. "I'm coming to you. You're exhausted, Brooke. You don't have to do this on your own. I'll be there in a few hours."

She hesitated, and I could hear the tension in her voice as she struggled to hold it together. "I don't want to drag you into this. You've got enough going on with the house, and Cody's fine with the sitter—"

"Brooke, I'm already packing a bag," I said, hoping it would push her to accept the help. "You need a break. And I want to be there for you. Cody's not the only one who needs you to be okay, you know?"

She let out a shaky laugh, but it didn't last long. "I just feel so out of control, Sean. I don't know what I'm doing anymore. I thought I could handle this job, but lately, it's like I'm failing at everything — work, being a mom, just…

everything."

"You're not failing at anything," I said firmly. "You're working hard, and you're doing the best you can. But it's okay to ask for help when you need it. You don't have to carry all of this alone."

There was a long pause, and I could hear her breathing, steadying herself. "I'm really sorry, Sean. I didn't mean to fall apart on you like this."

"Don't apologize," I said quickly. "You're allowed to feel this way. I'm just glad you called me. Now, promise me you'll leave the office and go home."

"I'll go home," she said softly. "I just… I feel like such a mess."

"We'll figure it out," I promised. "You're not alone in this. I'll help however I can. Just focus on getting home and resting for now. I'll be there as soon as I can."

"Okay," she whispered. "Thank you. I don't know what I'd do without you."

"You don't have to find out," I said with a smile. "I'm on my way."

She let out a long breath, and I could hear a little more calm in her voice. "Alright. I'll head home now. I'll see you soon?"

"Soon," I confirmed. "Just take care of yourself until I get there."

After we hung up, I stood there for a second, staring at the phone in my hand. Brooke never let herself fall apart like this, not around me, not around anyone. The fact that she was so close to breaking down told me just how much pressure she'd been under. And I wasn't about to let her go through it alone.

There was no time to waste. Brooke needed me, and I was going to be there, no matter what.

Finished and eager for early access to my next book? Check out my Patreon: patreon.com/jackbryce

THANK YOU FOR READING!

If you enjoyed this book, please check out my other work on Amazon.

Be sure to **leave me a review on Amazon** to let me know if you liked this book! Like most independent authors, I use the feedback from your review to improve my work and to decide what to focus on next, so your review can make a difference.

If you want early access to my work, consider joining my Patreon (https://patreon.com/jackbryce)!

If you want to stay up-to-date on my releases, you can join my newsletter by entering the following link into any web browser: https://fierce-thinker-305.ck.page/45f709af30. You can also join my Discord, where the madness never ends… Join by entering the following invite manually in your browser or Discord app:

https://discord.gg/uqXaTMQQhr.

Jack Bryce's Books

Below you'll find a list of my work, all available through my author page on Amazon.

Mage of Waycross (ongoing series)

Mage of Waycross 1

Mage of Waycross 2

Sky Lord (completed series)

Sky Lord 1

Sky Lord 2

Sky Lord 3

Frontier Summoner (completed series)

Frontier Summoner 1

Frontier Summoner 2

Frontier Summoner 3

Frontier Summoner 4

Frontier Summoner 5

Frontier Summoner 6

Frontier Summoner 7

Frontier Summoner 8

Frontier Summoner 9

Country Mage (completed series)

Country Mage 1

Country Mage 2

Country Mage 3

Country Mage 4

Country Mage 5

Country Mage 6

Country Mage 7

Country Mage 8

Country Mage 9

Country Mage 10

Aerda Online (completed series)

Phylomancer

Demon Tamer

Clanfather

Warped Earth (completed series)

Apocalypse Cultivator 1

Apocalypse Cultivator 2

Apocalypse Cultivator 3

Apocalypse Cultivator 4

Apocalypse Cultivator 5

Highway Hero (completed series)

Highway Hero 1

Highway Hero 2

Highway Hero 3

A SPECIAL THANKS TO...

My patron in the Godlike tier: Lynderyn!

My patron in the Archmage tier: James Hunt!

My patrons in the High Mage Tier: Brian M., David D., Eduardo P., and Walter Kimberly!

All of my other patrons at patreon.com/jackbryce!

Scott D., Louis Wu, and Joe M. for beta reading. You guys are absolute kings.

If you're interested in beta reading for me, hit me up on discord (JauntyHavoc#8836) or send an e-mail to lordjackbryce@gmail.com. The list is currently full, but that might change at any moment!

Made in United States
Troutdale, OR
12/29/2024

27365841R00246